I0762252

THE MIX-UP

THE MIX-UP

EVE MARIAN

Paige Publishing

April 2022 First Edition

ISBN-eBook: 978-1-7780262-2-5
ISBN-paperback: 978-1-7780262-1-8
ISBN-hardcover: 978-1-7780262-6-3

Contents

Content Warning

Scenes alluding to past trauma, one scene of domestic violence, a power imbalance, foul language, and open-door romance. Reader discretion is advised.

I

Frances

Standing inside the mailroom where I worked, I peered through the door's narrow window, watching the suits rush to the elevators to start their day. I was invisible to them. My coworkers in the mailroom barely knew my name, and outside this room, no one noticed me at all. That was just fine by me.

"Hey, you, can you take this up to the twelfth floor?" asked the manager, Clive, handing me a pile of packages. I nearly stumbled from the weight when he dropped them into my arms. He missed my struggle, having already turned his back to talk with his buddy.

I held the envelopes against my chest and pushed the door open with my back. The white marble foyer and stainless-steel doors of Crawford Corporation greeted me. As people hurried about, I avoided walking into their paths. Balancing the boxes, I struggled to press the elevator button. A man wearing a tight navy-blue suit studied his phone next to me. When the doors opened, he walked in first and pressed the button for the tenth floor.

"Twelfth floor, please," I said over the pile of mail.

Either ignoring me or having not heard me, he didn't move, his eyes glued to his phone. I shimmied to the front of the elevator and leaned forward until my index finger pressed the number twelve. Most people didn't pay attention to their surroundings, but I did.

Blowing a curl out of my face, I leaned back and waited for my floor.

When the doors opened, the familiar white marble desk with this week's avant-garde floral arrangement, stood in the center. At the desk sat the twelfth-floor receptionist, and my best friend Erika. She wore a bright yellow dress and her dark hair was pulled back into a sleek ponytail. A brilliant smile spread across her face when she saw me—a hint of a snicker on her lips. "That pile is nearly as tall as you."

"Yeah, and probably weighs just as much," I said, dropping the packages onto her desk. She rummaged through the pile efficiently, making separate stacks.

"Thank goodness there's nothing here for Crawford," she said, sorting through the last piece of mail.

Colton Crawford was Crawford Corporation's CEO and every employee's worst nightmare. Everyone had a story of when Colton Crawford had yelled or glared at them—everyone except for me. Unsurprisingly, he had never spoken to me. We rarely crossed paths, but someone in my position wouldn't interest a man like Crawford, anyway.

While most employees saw the CEO, I watched the man. Each morning, he dropped money into the homeless guy's cup, and whenever he grabbed a coffee in the lobby café, he tipped the barista every time.

"He's not that bad," I mumbled.

"Easy for you to say. You don't have to work with him."

Erika's hands clasped the mail as her eyes darted past my shoulder. "Shh, here he comes."

I swiveled to watch Colton approach us. A charcoal gray suit framed his tall and lean body. Every time he walked past me, he seemed to move in slow motion, like the hero in a Hollywood movie. His suit jacket flapped at his sides, revealing a broad chest and slim waist in a white buttoned shirt. I gripped my side, clenching my oversized sweater, as my stomach did a small flip. A whiff of designer cologne wafted past. I closed my eyes, imagining what the cologne would taste like if I were to press my lips to his neck.

"Cancel my eleven o'clock, Erika," said Colton as he punched the elevator button. I stared at the back of his short, dark hair.

"But, sir, she's already here," Erika said.

The doors opened, and Colton walked through them. Pivoting to face us, his face blank of any expression, he said, "I don't care," just as the mirrored doors punctuated his exit.

I sighed, and so did Erika. Only hers had a bit of a growl to it. "That's the second time this week he's canceled an interview at the last minute. How's he ever going to hire a new PA if he doesn't take the time to interview one?"

"What happened to his last personal assistant?" I asked, taking a deep breath to inhale the last remnants of Colton's cologne.

"The same thing that happened to the one before and the one before that. She got fed up with his rude remarks and short temper and quit."

Walking around the desk with a stack of mail under her arm, Erika turned just as she proceeded down the hallway. "Meet you downstairs for lunch?"

I smiled. "See you soon."

The air in the elevator was thick with his bergamot scent, and I unabashedly basked in it, twirling in the closed space with my arms outstretched like some fairy in a field. Unfortunately, when the doors opened, I was no longer alone but staring at a crowd of suits. No one had noted my foolishness, distracted by their files and phones. I scurried through them and wandered back to the mailroom.

Clive and the others chatted while they sorted through packages. I checked my phone and saw a message from my brother, Marco. At eighteen, Marco was eight years my junior.

Marco: Won't be home for dinner. Meeting after school, then taking a shift at the supermarket. I'll be home by 11:00.

I shot a quick text back: K. Don't work too hard.

Ironic that message. We had no choice but to work hard. Our parents immigrated to Syracuse, New York when they married twenty-five years ago. They worked two jobs, leaving my grandmother to raise us. She didn't speak any English at the time but fortunately taught us Italian. When Marco and I were old enough, we got jobs to help out, too.

Glancing up at the clock, I realized it was nearly noon and time for lunch. I grabbed my knapsack and walked outside toward Katy's Deli. Scanning the room, I didn't see Erika, so I chose a table near the back. Although we met here for lunch nearly every day, I never ordered, instead brought my own sandwich to save money. I hoped she'd arrive any minute, otherwise, they'd probably kick me out soon.

A few minutes later, I spotted her yellow dress at the order desk and relaxed my shoulders. She hurried toward me.

"Ugh, I don't have much time. My afternoon is packed with meetings and I have to be there to greet everyone."

"That's okay," I said, taking a bite of my pastrami sandwich. "I have a busy afternoon, too."

Erika watched me eat my sandwich with one eyebrow raised. "Really?"

"Yep," I said, wiping my mouth with a napkin I'd brought from home.

"Frannie, when will you wake up and realize you're too good for that job?"

She asked me this at least once a week, so I didn't bother answering.

"You have a college degree in business," she continued. "You can do a lot more with that than working with Clive."

I nodded and took another bite of my sandwich. Erika already knew my story, but she insisted on giving me this speech all the time. "You know I can't quit. I need this job."

"I'm not telling you to quit right away, but to find something better." She smiled and leaned back in her chair. "Why don't you apply for the PA position?"

Horrified, I nearly choked on my lunch, coughing out a piece of bread. "Are you crazy?" I said. "I couldn't work under Colton." A smile played on my lips. "Well, maybe I could work *under* him."

Erika cringed. "Whatever you see in that man, I've no idea. He's such a jerk."

"I can't take that job," I said more definitively.

"Why not? You're more than qualified for it."

Shaking my head, I took another bite. "I've no experience, so no chance of getting the position."

"You used that excuse right out of college."

"Well, it still applies now."

Erika watched me and I stretched the collar of my sweater, her words tightening around my throat. Too humiliated to admit it scared me to want something badly and fail, I looked down at the menu instead.

"All right. I'll let this go if you promise me you'll look at the position my cousin has at the mall. You'd be a manager there, and the pay is better than the mailroom."

The thought of meeting new people and interviewing for a new position sat like a piece of lead in my stomach. I knew we could use the money to get Marco into his graphic arts program, but we were doing just fine. We were getting by and could afford the first-semester payment thanks to his after-school job. There was no reason I should have to quit and find something new. "Thanks, Erika. I know you're trying to help. But I'm comfortable in the mailroom. It suits me."

She sighed. "I just know you are meant for more than this, that's all."

I glimpsed down at my white sneakers and black tights. I liked not having to dress up to go to work. I didn't need anything more than what I had. A small voice inside me asked, *do you want more?* But I ignored it. The last time I wanted more, I'd been punished for it. So, I'd learned to be quiet and satisfied with what I had. The coping mechanism had worked for the past six years. Why would I want to change that?

It made me feel safe.

"Are you trying to get rid of me?" I teased, wanting to change the subject.

"Nah, you're the best thing about Crawford Corp," she laughed and took a bite of her veggie sandwich.

"You're not so bad yourself," I smiled back.

As we walked back to the office a little while later, a deep voice stopped us as soon as we entered the building.

"You're late," Colton said, walking past Erika toward the elevators. He held a briefcase in one hand and checked his watch with the other. He removed his jacket, and I could see the muscles on his back straining as he walked away from us.

"So are you, jackass," she murmured when he was out of earshot. I couldn't hold back my snort. Erika squeezed my hand, concerned Colton would hear me, but she didn't have to worry. He just kept on walking.

"I'll see you later," she said, and gave my hand one last squeeze.

Standing there, watching him, I pictured myself following

Colton into the elevator and telling him how I dreamt of him every night. He'd laugh and scoop me up in his arms. I sighed and wiped the goofy smile from my lips before returning to the mailroom. I was a few minutes late, but Clive didn't yell at me. He was too busy talking about last night's game.

Just as I dropped my knapsack, my phone buzzed. It was a message from my brother.

Marco: Looks like I'll be home for dinner. The supermarket laid a bunch of us, part-timers, off. ☹

What?

I read his message again, checking to make sure I'd read it right the first time.

Crap. What now?

Mom and Dad already worked two jobs and the grocery hours worked best for Marco's school schedule.

My shoulders slumped with the added burden.

What should I do?

The afternoon dragged on and the guilt of knowing I could help Marco, but I was too afraid to do it, gnawed at me.

Come on, Frances. You were never like this. You used to challenge yourself in college. But that was before... him.

I pressed down on my lips and pushed the memories away.

Grabbing my phone, I opened a new text for Erika.

Me: Send me the info for the mall position.

2

Colton

Where are those files that I asked for?

Damn it, I'd forgotten again that my last PA quit. I didn't have time to look for another one.

I pressed the intercom button for one of our accountants. "Daniel, bring me the Robert Morgan file." Daniel remained silent on the other end, but I knew he'd do it. He always did, albeit grumbling.

A few minutes later, my brother Ryan strolled into my office, carrying a yellow file folder. "Here," he said, dropping the file on my desk.

"I asked Daniel to bring it to me. This isn't your job." As a lawyer, Ryan led the legal department at Crawford Corp. I picked up the file anyway and leafed through it.

"It's not his job either," he said, dropping into the black leather armchair in front of my desk and crossing his arms. "When are you going to hire a new assistant?"

"Soon. I just have a million other things to do first." I found the report I was looking for and pulled it from the file.

Leaning forward with his forearm on my desk, Ryan asked, "So, how was your date last night? I saw the pictures all over the internet this morning."

I sighed, knowing he wasn't kidding. "It was a one and done."

"Ouch, that's harsh. What happened?"

"The same thing that happens every time. She talked little, looked down at her phone often, and worked her way into my pants quickly."

Ryan raised an eyebrow. "That's the first time I've heard you complain about any woman putting her hands on you."

"Yeah, well, if I didn't think she was sticking her hand down there to look for my wallet, I may have been a little more flattered."

"Sucks when your wallet is more impressive than your package," he snickered.

I glared at him. "You know that's not it. I'm just sick of all these fake, lying, plastic girls."

"So go find yourself a real woman." Ryan leaned back in the armchair. "But those women take time and effort."

"No, thanks. I'll just avoid dating altogether."

Ryan barked out a laugh. "Yeah, right. You haven't gone two days without sex."

"Yes, I have. Don't be ridiculous."

Ryan grinned. "I bet you can't go two months without dating a woman."

Two months! My face must have shown my horror because Ryan fell over laughing.

"That's what I thought. You know, you're just as fake as them. You say you want complex, but really you want it easy. Just admit the truth. You can't do it."

"Aren't we a little old for one of your dumb bets?" I sighed.

"They're only dumb to you because you always lose." He chuckled.

I wanted to shut Ryan's cocky mouth. He constantly went on about how he was the smartest one in the family and always knew what to do before any of us had a chance to step in. Having graduated with a law degree, he rarely lost an argument. He also wasn't the one responsible for what happened to us when we were children. *I was.*

I stood, placing my hands on my desk. "Two months? No sex?"

He stood too. "No sex. No touching. Nothing."

"What do I get if I win?"

He shrugged. "Your pride?"

"Nah, I've already got that. I want your house in Cabo."

Ryan sucked in his lips, considering my request. "Fine. But if I win, which I will, I get your Lamborghini."

He knew how much I loved that car. I had it specially ordered from Italy. But I would not lose this time. "Fine," I said.

He threw out his hand and we shook on it.

Frances

"Well, well, well. Look at you, Ms. Frances Netto." Erika gave a little whistle.

I smoothed out my fitted white blouse and black pencil skirt. "I didn't have time to go home and change after the job interview."

Her eyes twinkled as she continued to smile at me. "I like this new look on you."

"Thanks, but don't get used to it," I said. "I wanted to impress your friend at the mall and only wore this hoping it would help me land the position."

"How did the interview go?"

"Really well, I think."

"I'm proud of you, Frannie. I know it wasn't easy for you." She squeezed my hand.

Erika knew some of what happened in my past, but no one really knew the entire story. I didn't like talking about it.

"See you at Katy's," I said. But as I walked back to the elevator, I remembered something.

"Oh, Erika. The envelope on top is for Crawford. He needs to sign for it. The sender wants proof of receipt. You can bring it to me at lunch." I turned and took only one step before Erika stopped me.

"Oh, no. No way. I'm not going in there today. He's been crusty all morning."

"You have to," I said.

"No, I don't. If you need the signature, then you need to get it." Erika pointed her finger toward the end of the hallway at Colton's office.

"Please. For me, will you go in there and get the signature?"

"Frances, I would walk through hot coals for you, but I won't go into that office today."

"Fine," I said, realizing I was making a bigger deal about it than necessary. "He probably won't notice me, anyway."

Erika looked me up and down. "Oh, he'll notice you."

Rolling my eyes at her, I grabbed the envelope from her desk and marched to the end of the hallway. I slowed my pace when I nearly reached Colton's office. Closing my eyes, I raised my fist and knocked on his door.

No answer. But the door creaked open and his desk sat empty. Poking my head in, I checked the room and didn't see him. Should I just drop the envelope on his desk and tell Clive that I personally delivered the package myself? That was proof enough, wasn't it?

Not sure why I tiptoed to his desk, but I did and planned to scurry out of his office as quickly as I could when something on his desk caught my eye.

Ava Grady. Her name was in bold and underlined, with a blue and violet logo stamped underneath. I picked up the paper, realizing it was a resume, and studied it. It looked great and I thought perhaps I could do something similar to my resume. If I didn't get the job at the mall, I would need to find something soon.

Scanning the page, I noticed Ava attended the same program in college as me, only she hadn't graduated with honors. I grimaced; it was petty of me to notice. Looking down the page, I read that she belonged to a Youth Group at her church and served as President for three years. Her resume had a lot more extra-curricular activities than mine did, but we were similarly qualified. Maybe Erika was right and I should apply for a PA position. Definitely not this one, as I wouldn't want to work for someone I imagined naked at least once a day. But maybe somewhere else.

"What are you doing in here?" A deep voice called from the side of the room.

I jumped, clutching the paper to my chest. I opened my mouth, but Colton Crawford's incredulous face as he stared at me rendered me speechless. His gaze raked across my body until his eyes landed on the paper. He walked over and plucked it from my hands.

"Ow," I hissed, shaking my hand. A faint red line sliced through my index finger, and I instinctively put it in my mouth and sucked. His eyes followed my movement. I felt the heat behind them and dropped my hand, as though burnt by his stare.

Leaving him to read the resume, I turned toward the door.

"Wait," he called.

I halted, prepared for his scolding, an apology ready on my lips.

"Take a seat, Ms. Grady."

Ms. Grady?

Still holding the paper in his hand, he said, "Look. I won't waste both our time with interviews. Your resume looks fine, and frankly, what I need to know about you will come through your work, not your words. When can you start?"

"Oh, no," I said, shaking my head. "I'm not. I mean, I didn't come here for..."

"Right. You came to talk about salary. I understand how these interviews work." He took a seat at his desk. "The position pays eighty grand a year to start, with benefits. You can go over the details with Frank in HR."

"What? Eighty thousand?" I asked, certain I hadn't heard him correctly. "You're kidding, right?" That was more than double what I made in the mailroom.

"I wasn't. But I don't have time to waste, Ms. Grady," he said, running a hand through his hair. "One hundred thousand, but I need you to start tomorrow. Can you do that?"

One hundred thousand dollars. Holy Mother of... gah! That would take years for me to earn, and he was offering it to me in twelve months. Well, to Ava Grady.

I couldn't take the job. I wasn't Ava Grady. But that money would pay for Marco's entire college career and clear my own debt. No. I couldn't lie, and especially not for an entire year.

What if it were only for two weeks? A voice whispered in my head.

That first two-week paycheck would be enough to pay for Marco's first semester. We'll figure out the rest later, but it would be enough for now. Two weeks, ten business days. I could keep up the pretense for that long.

"One hundred thousand," I said. "And I need the first paycheck in cash." I certainly couldn't cash a cheque made out to an Ava Grady.

He tilted his head. "Are there any illegal activities I need to know about?"

"No," I squeaked, then steadied my voice. "Still settling some things with my bank."

He tossed the resume into the wastebasket and turned toward his computer. "Fine. You start tomorrow," he said, and began typing, rudely dismissing me.

"Tomorrow," I repeated as I smoothed down my skirt and turned to leave.

"Ms. Grady," he called.

I slowly turned to face him and held my voice steady. "Yes?"

"Welcome to Crawford Corporation," he said and cleared his throat. He continued to stare at his screen while straightening his tie, his lips twitching as though it pained him to be nice.

I swallowed with difficulty. "Feels like I've already worked here for years," I said and rushed out before he read the truth written all over my face.

3

Frances

Erika's bulging eyes and open mouth would have been comical if I wasn't so terrified. We were sitting at Katy's deli and I'd just told her what I'd done. When I'd left Colton's office, I was too scared to stop and speak to Erika in case he came out and overheard us.

"You did what?" she asked for the second time.

I inhaled a deep breath and closed my eyes. "I took the PA position."

"But you didn't apply for the position."

"I know. It was a mix-up. When I held Ava Grady's resume in my hand, he thought I was her."

"I don't know about this, Frances," she said, staring at me.

"I just have to keep up the ruse for two weeks, then I'll quit," I said.

"And I'm supposed to pretend that I don't know you?"

"Yes."

She shook her head. "This sounds like trouble."

Yes. Big trouble. What the heck was I thinking? Maybe it wasn't too late to call it off. But then what? I still didn't have a plan to help Marco. I couldn't let him down when there was something I could do to help him. And maybe, well, maybe there'd be something in it for me, too. "With the experience, I'll feel more comfortable applying for PA positions with my real name."

She blew out a breath. "I don't like this, Frannie. You're a terrible liar. Remember when we tried to sneak those boys up into your room?"

"Are you kidding? My grandmother would have killed us."

"What about when you tried to return those shoes and the clerk asked if you'd worn them and you'd said, 'only once'?"

I twisted my lips. "This isn't the same thing."

"No. It's worse. You could lose your job."

She was right, but I wasn't turning back now. "I'm doing this for Marco because I would do anything for him. Besides, you know better than I do, Colton Crawford rarely speaks to his assistants. He just barks orders at them. I only have to stay quiet and get the work done. I can manage that." I was trying to convince Erika as much as myself.

Erika pursed her lips, then exhaled loudly. "Fine. But stay away from him as much as you can."

"I will," I said, then my eyes caught a tall figure at the deli's entrance. "Oh, god!"

I grabbed the laminated menu on the table and raised it, covering my face. I sensed Erika turn around and heard her say, "Fate may have other plans, though."

"What's he doing here, anyway?" I hissed.

"Man's gotta eat, too."

"Yes, but we've never seen him in here before."

"Looks like he's trying something new," said Erika, her voice carrying over the loud conversations around us. "Wait. That's strange."

"What is?" I asked.

"He's not in line to order. It looks, well, he's straining his neck. It seems as though he's looking for someone."

"Who?"

"How the heck should I know?" She paused. "Oh, boy," groaned Erika.

"What?"

"I think he saw me," she said.

"Oh, no!" I cried.

"Don't worry. It's not like he's... Oh shit. He's coming over here."

I tried to sink lower into my seat, but it was useless. My cheeks burned, anticipating his reaction to seeing me here with Erika.

"Hello," said Colton, his deep voice cutting through the loud lunch crowd. "Surprised to see you here, Erika."

"Strange. I eat here every day."

"You do?" Although it was a question, his voice didn't seem interested in the answer. Instead, I felt his eyes on me. I knew I should say hello, but I just needed another minute to get my embarrassment under control.

"Is that you, Ms. Grady?" he asked.

My heart hammered in my chest and I could barely take a full breath. I lowered the menu and smiled weakly.

"I thought that was you walking into this place," he said, crossing his arms.

Erika tilted her head and narrowed her eyes at him. "You followed her here?"

"Not exactly," he said, shooting a glare at Erika. Straightening his tie, he turned back to me. "I forgot to tell you that I need you to start early tomorrow. Eight o'clock sharp."

I nodded. "Not a problem."

I prayed for him to leave quickly, but he just stood there, studying me. Oh no, here it comes. Then he fixed his gaze on Erika and back to me. "How do you two know each other?" he asked, waving a finger between us.

I gulped. Erika was right. I couldn't go through with the lie. I couldn't deny knowing her. Time to confess, and I hadn't even made it to the first day. Dropping the menu onto the table, I looked him in the eye. "She's my friend. She asked me to apply for the position—"

He put his hands in his pockets, raising his suit's lapels. Turning to Erika, he said. "Good work, Ms. Jackson." He grinned at her with a smile that would have melted my panties had he given it to me.

Erika swallowed and nodded just as Colton tapped the table and left us sitting there, both of our mouths open.

"Damn," said Erika. "He's hot when he's not being a jackass."

I nodded in agreement.

She shook her head and smiled. "Lying with the truth. Not bad. Maybe you can make this work after all."

"Of course, I can," I said, and knew I was still lying through my teeth.

Walking back to Crawford Corp, I knew I had one more lie to tell that day, and it was to Clive. My hands trembled, so I stuffed them into my coat pockets.

"I need to take my two weeks' vacation, starting tomorrow," I said. I thought my voice had cracked, but Clive hadn't noticed.

"Tomorrow? But that's Thursday. Just start on Monday."

Ugh, what do I say now? Think, Frances.

"No. My grandmother's ill and I need to stay home and take care of her." *Nonna* would kill me if she heard me use her health in vain. *I'm sorry, Nonna.* "Besides, I haven't taken a holiday in two years. I really need this now."

Clive sucked his teeth. He knew that was true. I hadn't taken a vacation last year or the year before, opting to take a lump cash reimbursement for the time off instead. *Please say yes, please!*

"Fine," he said. "But next time, give me some notice, why don't you."

My lungs emptied and I nearly dropped to the ground in relief. "I will. I promise."

I wasn't worried about bumping into Clive. He rarely left the mailroom and the others barely knew I existed. I was worried about working for Colton. I'd heard everyone's complaints about him and now I'd just agreed to be his assistant. Me. The person who wants to be invisible can't hide from him now.

What the heck did I get myself into?

***

I woke up early, knowing I'd need the extra time to choose my work clothes. It was early December and the weather had already turned cold. Staring longingly at my tights, I trudged past them to my mother's closet.

I pulled out a black shift dress, but my eyes wandered to the curve-hugging tan dress I'd worn years ago. I loved how it fit, but I didn't want any extra attention on Ava Grady. So, I grabbed the simple black one instead.

I arrived at the office at seven-thirty. I knew which desk in the long row of cubicles belonged to Colton's PA and settled in. Turning on the laptop, I cleared out the previous PA's old emails and created a signature for my outgoing messages. I opened Colton's calendar and saw that he had several meetings booked for the day, but left only a thirty-minute window for lunch.

I should order him something.

I was just about to grab a coffee when Colton strode down the hallway. He wore a dark blue suit today with a white shirt and navy tie. His brown shoes matched his belt and he looked like he was ready for his close-up. I bit my lip while my eyes took in every stitch of that fine Italian suit.

His lush green eyes met mine and one side of his lips pulled up. Miraculously, my panties were intact.

"Good morning, Mr. Crawford," I said, standing from my desk.

He stepped into his office and waved me to follow him. I grabbed my notepad and pencil and took a seat in front of his desk. The back of my legs hit the soft black leather, and I couldn't help but wonder what it would feel like to straddle him in this chair. *Focus Frances!*

Colton tilted his head and his lips turned into a full smirk.

Sweet Lordy, did my face just give away my inappropriate thoughts? I hoped not, but a familiar heat crept up my neck and scorched my face.

"Please, call me Colton." He took off his suit jacket and unbuttoned the first button underneath his tie. My eyes lingered on his neck.

I cleared my throat twice and pushed back my hair. I should have tied it up instead of leaving the curls loose past my shoulders. I crossed my legs and raised my notebook onto my knee. "Yes, Colton. Where would you like to start?"

4

Colton

I'd like to start by running my hand from your bare ankle to your knee, to your sweet... I shook my head, dismissing the thought.

I'd never lost focus at work, not until Ms. Ava Grady showed up. It had been barely five minutes since she'd walked into my office, and I already wanted to rip that notebook from her hands and put my mouth on every inch of her body.

That's not happening, Colton.

Not only because I bet Ryan I could stay away from women for two months, but because she's my personal assistant and I never, ever, mixed business with pleasure.

"Let's start with today's schedule, Ms. Grady," I said instead.

"You can call me Ava." Even her name made me feel guilty. It sounded like a prayer or a dark angel tempting me to give in to my urges.

"Good," I continued. "Now, I have several meetings today, but only one is important."

She raised her pencil and held it over her paper, waiting for my direction. "I have a two o'clock meeting with a Mr. Robert Morgan. It's imperative that this meeting go well."

She scribbled on her notepad. "Is this the same Robert Morgan from Morgan and Sons?" she asked.

I folded my hands on my desk, impressed that she was familiar with the company since only a few outside of our industry were. She must have done some research for this position. "Yes. I need him to sell me the land he owns on Main and First streets."

She looked up. "Why?"

Don't bark at her. You need this one to stay.

"It's not your job to ask why. You just need to know this deal must happen. Your job is to take notes while Morgan is here and ensure he is comfortable. We will debrief after the meeting for anything I'll need you to follow up on. Understood?"

Talking business brought me back to my old self again and I liked it better this way. I was sure-footed—always knew which steps to take next.

"Understood." She waited for further instruction. There were a few other things I wanted to tell her, but none had anything to do with her job.

"Good. You may go," I said, dismissing her. "Have Erika set up your email and show you around the company's private file folders."

A tiny smile played on her lips. "Will do."

When she stood and turned away from my desk, my eyes fell to her perfectly rounded ass. I didn't know what it was about her that had me imagining new positions and angles. She was pretty, but I'd turned down pretty many times. There was a quiet elegance about her that drew me in, and I wanted to know if I could make her scream.

"Knock, knock," Ryan called from the doorway, rapping his knuckles lightly on the door. He stepped into my office but only had eyes for Ava.

"Hi, there. I'm Ryan Crawford." He raised his hand forward and slapped on his best shit-eating grin.

"Ava Grady," she said, smiling back.

Ryan held her hand a little longer than necessary and the bastard even wet his lips.

"That is all, Ava," I said from my desk. My voice had carried louder than I'd expected. Her shoulders straightened, but she left the room without a word.

"You were rude," said Ryan, still watching her as she walked back to her desk.

"You were eye fucking my PA," I shot back.

Ryan laughed. "Not exactly. I'd only gotten as far as undressing her with my eyes."

"Well, knock it off. We don't mess around with employees."

Ryan sat in the armchair across from me and smiled his stupid-ass smile.

"What?" I barked, turning on my laptop.

"You're already in a bad mood and it's not even nine o'clock. You didn't get laid last night, did you?"

"Of course not. I have a bet to win. Besides, I'm not interested right now, anyway."

That was a lie.

"Well, I'm very interested. How good is that PA? Any chance she'll quit soon?"

"Back off, Ryan," I said. "She started today and I don't have time to look for a new one. I've got a meeting with Morgan this afternoon."

That seemed to distract my brother. "Really? How did you accomplish that?"

I'd slept with Morgan's PA and she penciled me in right after I gave her the best sex of her life. Her words, not mine. "I simply made an appointment."

"Sure," he said. "And I'm still a virgin."

I shook my head. *Yeah, right.*

Since we were teenage boys, my brothers and I only wanted one thing more than getting out of our foster parents' house, and that was sex. Blessed with our birth father's last name and good looks, it was never a problem. Until our exploits started hitting the tabloids, then we all agreed to be discreet about it. No one liked it when a client brought up the morning's headline at a meeting.

"Is there a reason for your visit, Ryan?" I asked, reopening my schedule for the day.

"Yes. I came to tell you that Luke wants to host a dinner at his place next week. You should be there, Colton."

Luke had remodeled and now lived in the home we grew up in before our parents died in a car accident. I hadn't been back at the house since I was nine years old.

"You can't keep avoiding it," he said. Then, in a softer voice, "You were just a kid. We never held you responsible for what happened."

"Not yet," I said, and opened an internet browser. "I'm close to fixing the past. But not yet."

Even though I faced away from him, I felt his eyes on me. "Don't turn him down," said Ryan. "Promise me you'll think about it."

The thought of disappointing my baby brother didn't sit well with me, so I conceded a little. "I'll think about it."

Standing, Ryan knocked on my desk and walked over to my door. "I think I'll stop by the new girl's desk and make sure she's settling in all right."

"Stay away from my assistant," I shouted.

Ryan laughed and walked right past Ava, but not without giving her a nod. Even from this distance, I noticed a blush creep onto her cheeks. She'd done the same at the deli. I wondered if she was the type that blushed with every emotion, be it anger, embarrassment... excitement. Did it spread down her neck and lower? I groaned. I was entirely too distracted by my PA. It would be much easier if I could take her out, give her the best night of her life, then get her out of my head.

Stupid bet. Stupid company rules.

I swiveled my chair to face my laptop again and typed the address of an auction site I checked regularly into the search bar. Nothing. I tried another site, then the last one. Still nothing. I rubbed the back of my neck, feeling my muscles tighten. Twenty years—and I was still searching for two more pieces of jewelry. Then it would be over. Then I could return to my parents' home.

By eleven, Ava had brought me up to speed with the latest client reports. She had itemized the ones that needed my immediate attention and had taken notes while I shot back the calls to action for her to handle. I didn't have to slow down or repeat myself. She had kept her nose down and scribbled on her notepad. Then, when I sent her an email to look into last year's numbers and get back to me by the end of the day, she hadn't told me I was unreasonable. No. She sent me an email with all the information before lunch.

A part of me was disappointed. She was really good at her job. And other than keeping to herself, I didn't seem to intimidate her. She wouldn't quit today, and probably not tomorrow either. I had to learn to think of Ms. Ava Grady as just my assistant.

I checked the time. It was nearly noon and I had another call starting in a half-hour. It wouldn't be enough time to grab my usual coffee and a bagel, so I decided to head downstairs and buy a coffee from the café inside the lobby.

"I'll be back in thirty minutes," I told Ava as I walked past her desk for lunch. She was on the phone, so I didn't expect a response.

Walking past the front desk receptionist, I said, "Have a good lunch, Erika."

She stared at me as though I'd spoken a foreign language. Then she peeked down the hall. "You too, Mr. Crawford," she said, rising from her seat.

As the elevator doors closed, I spotted Ava hurrying toward me.

"Wait!" she called.

I pressed the button to hold the doors open.

Her chest heaved as she raced to reach me, and I glued my gaze to her face or else risked rushing up to her and truly taking her breath away. I banished the image of a panting and naked Ava Grady.

"I ordered your lunch," she said when she'd finally caught her breath.

"You did?" I'd heard of other PAs ordering lunch for their bosses, but it had never happened to me before. I'd also never trusted any of them to not poison me.

"Yes. Coffee and a bagel. It will be here any minute. You're probably holding up the elevator."

"How did you know what I eat for lunch?"

Her eyes darted to Erika and then back to me. "I asked Erika yesterday."

Turning to Erika, I noticed the woman's eyes narrow, but then she smiled. "Yes. She did."

"I didn't realize you paid so much attention to my eating habits, Ms. Jackson."

"Neither did I," she murmured.

As I stepped off the elevator, a man holding a coffee opened the door to the stairwell.

"Hey, Fran—"

"Oh, good! Your lunch is here." Ava raced toward the man.

"Yeah, I had to take the stairs. The elevator wasn't working."

Ava grabbed the coffee and tapped her foot while he pulled a brown paper bag from his carrier. "I'll see you later," she said, and pushed him toward the stairs and closed the door.

I turned to Erika, wondering if I was the only one who thought Ava's behavior quite strange. But Erika didn't look up, focused on her keyboard.

"Should I put this on your meeting desk?" asked Ava with a smile, but her eyes shifted between Erika and the empty stairwell.

"Sure," I said, wondering what the heck that was all about.

I watched her saunter away from me, her skirt hugging every curve. When she reached my office, she removed the items from the bag and placed them on the desk.

"What about you, Ava? Did you not order something for yourself?"

"No. I brought my lunch."

"Why don't you join me then?"

She sucked in her lips and looked down the hallway. "Um." She seemed to ponder the question longer than I thought necessary. "I really shouldn't."

"It's just lunch," I told her.

"All right. Just give me a minute. I usually go to lunch with Erika."

"Usually? But this is your first day."

Her eyes rounded, and she swallowed hard. "Ah... I mean... I planned to go to lunch with Erika since we met up at the Deli yesterday. I'll just go tell her I can't make it."

I nodded but found her explanation strange. My new assistant was a little jumpy. Taking a sip of my coffee, I sat down at the desk. Ava and Erika looked to be arguing. Erika's hands were on her hips while Ava ran her fingers through her hair. Finally, Erika grabbed her purse and stormed toward the elevators. I couldn't look away from the scene. Then Ava stopped her and squeezed Erika's hand before letting her go. She'd mentioned the two of them were friends.

Is there more between them than just friendship?

"Is there something going on between you and Erika?" I asked when she returned holding a floral pink reusable bag.

She stopped mid-step. "What do you mean?"

"Just that you two seem very close. Is there something I should know?"

Her cheeks reddened and she pushed a curl behind her ear. "No. There's nothing you need to know."

Huh. I think I was just dismissed. She was right, of course. It was none of my business, but dammit, I wanted to know if I had a shot.

What are you talking about? She's your assistant. There is no shot to take.

Ava sat down and pulled out a container with three slices of pizza in it. I smiled when she closed her eyes before taking the first bite. The last woman I'd dated ordered the most expensive item on the menu but didn't even take a bite of it. It had bothered me. Not only the waste but also the disconnection.

I found it comforting to share a meal with someone else. When we were younger, my brothers and I always ate dinner together. Our foster parents were rarely there, but we always sat down in front of some makeshift meal. Even though Luke was the baby, he was the one who enjoyed cooking the most. When I was old enough to work, I would pick up something special, like veal sandwiches, for the three of us on Friday nights.

I watched Ava pick up her slice with her unpainted fingernails and bring it to her pink mouth. Her lipstick had worn off, but her mouth beckoned me, nonetheless.

"Would you like a bite?" she asked.

"Excuse me?"

"You were staring at my pizza."

I was staring at your mouth, actually. But I couldn't tell her that.

"No. I'm good. I was just wondering where you ordered it from. It looks good."

"Oh, it's homemade."

"You made it?"

"Gosh, no. My grandmother did. She's an amazing cook."

"You live with your grandmother?"

"Yes. And my parents and brother."

Huh. That surprised me. It'd been a long while since I'd spoken to a woman who still lived at home with her parents. While I would have thought it'd make her less sophisticated, I found it quite endearing, actually. Not having a proper family life, I envied her. I probably wouldn't want to leave a happy home either.

"You must like living at home," I said.

Her cheeks reddened and I wanted to take the words back. I hadn't meant them as an insult, but I couldn't help thinking I'd hurt her feelings.

"I mean, you must have a great family."

"I do," she said but didn't elaborate.

She remained quiet for some minutes and I'd lost any hope of carrying on with the conversation, until she said, "Sometimes... all you have is family."

She stared down at her pizza, but her words hit me square in the chest. I owned a large penthouse, a multi-billion-dollar company, and fancy cars, but none of them mattered because I'd lost my family and lost what was precious to them.

"And when you lose it... you feel lost yourself."

Her eyelashes fluttered and she stared back at me. It was just one sentence, but I had revealed to her in those few words more about me than I'd even divulged to my brothers. I sipped my coffee and looked around the office. "So, what do you think of the job so far?"

She smiled. "I think it's great."

I laughed. "Well, I won't lie. You'd be the first one to think that."

"Why is that?" she asked, a mischievous smile playing on her lips.

"Because I can be an asshole."

Now it was her turn to laugh.

"I know it sounds crazy. But I can be difficult to work with," I teased. I couldn't believe I was teasing and laughing with my assistant. The most I'd ever hoped for was a competent employee. But I was starting to really like Ms. Ava Grady.

"Perhaps this time will be different."

It already was different. She was different.

We finished our lunch and Ava excused herself, saying she needed to check on a few things before we met with Robert Morgan.

I finalized my speaking points and knew I had Morgan where I needed him. But that didn't necessarily mean he'd sell me the property. Morgan was a gambler and he always bet on the underdog. I was not an underdog in this case, so I needed to impress him.

From the corner of my eye, I spotted Ava greeting a white-haired man wearing a blue pin-striped suit and yellow tie. The suit screamed bad taste, but Morgan was not one for fashion. He was all business. He kissed the back of Ava's hand and she blushed, the color imprinting in my mind. She ushered him into my office.

"Mr. Morgan. Wonderful to see you, sir," I said and shook his hand. "Please, take a seat."

He remained standing just inside my office. "I don't recall agreeing to this meeting, but my assistant insisted that I had."

Thank you, Diane.

"Well, you're a very busy man, sir. I'm sure it just slipped your mind."

He narrowed his eyes. "I don't recall this meeting because I would never have agreed to it. I don't plan on selling any of my properties. Not to you. Not to anyone. I came to tell you in person, so you'll stop harassing my assistant."

This was going to be harder than I thought. "I understand. But since you're already here, why don't you sit back and let me share some numbers with you?"

"I don't have time for this—"

Ava walked into my office holding a coffee and a small package. "Excuse me, Mr. Morgan?"

He turned toward her with his fists curled at his sides. "Yes?"

"I hope you don't mind the interruption, but I brought these cannoli for your meeting."

"What?" I asked.

What the hell is she thinking? Interrupting my meeting for some pastries?

"My grandmother made them last night." Her voice shook. "I understand homemade cannoli are your favorite, Mr. Morgan."

Morgan's mouth opened and I was certain it watered because he licked his lips as he stared at the white box in Ava's hand.

"My grandmother is Sicilian, so they're pretty authentic. But if you were heading out, I'll just put these in the lunchroom for the staff."

"No! I wasn't leaving. Not yet, at least."

She placed the cannoli on the meeting desk and I took my cue. "Why don't we all take a seat and chat over there," I suggested.

Morgan sat in front of the pastries faster than I'd thought possible. He groaned after taking a bite. "These are the best I've ever had," he said, polishing off the first one.

"I'll let my grandmother know," said Ava, a ghost of a smirk curled on her lips as she sat at the table with her notebook and pencil ready. *Holy Shit. She played him!*

I sat down in front of Morgan and took advantage of his excellent mood.

After an hour of going through my plan and what that would mean to Morgan's pockets, he finally stood up. "I'll have to think about it, Crawford."

"I understand. If there's anything you need to clarify, don't hesitate to contact me."

I shook his hand and walked him to the door.

"Mr. Morgan, before you go," Ava said as she grabbed something from her desk. She approached Morgan with another package, this time a white fancy lunch bag.

"I got these for Taylor. Your assistant mentioned they were his favorite."

Who?

"You did?" asked Morgan. "How very thoughtful of you."

She smiled. "I hope he enjoys them."

"Oh, I'm sure he will." He stuck out his hand and Ava shook it. "It was a pleasure meeting you."

"You as well," she said. "I hope we meet again soon."

Morgan turned to me and shook his finger at me. "You know. I think I pegged you all wrong, Crawford. If you were smart enough to hire her, you may not be an idiot after all."

"Thank you," I said, knowing his words were no compliment.

What the heck was inside that bag?

"I'll see you later," he called and walked down the hallway.

"What did you give him?" I asked when Morgan was in the elevator.

She smiled. "Doggy treats."

"You're joking?" I asked. She had to be kidding.

"After I spoke to his assistant about his favorite dessert, I went online and checked his social media profile. The man loves his dog more than his wife and kids, judging from all the pictures he takes with him. So, I called her back and asked if she knew Taylor's favorite treat, too."

Holy Shit. She's fucking brilliant.

I couldn't believe she'd thought to do all that. "You're amazing!" I said and moved closer to her. Her brown eyes flickered up and captured mine with a poignant gaze. I raised my hand toward her face, itching to pull her closer. Leaning in, I knew I would kiss her right here in the middle of the office. My fingers burrowed inside her hair. *Shit!*

Her eyes rounded, as large as saucers, as I pulled away. "I'm sorry. I shouldn't have done that," I said.

"It's… okay. We were excited. You didn't mean it."

Only I did mean it.

"Thank you, Ava," I said, my voice deepening.

She wet her lips. "You're welcome."

Then she turned and walked away.

5

Frances

The office holiday party was tonight and I didn't plan to attend. But Erika argued that I needed to get out more. Although we were both worried about me running into the mailroom employees, she assured me she'd watch my back.

I went to her apartment after work and she picked out a dress from her closet that screamed Ava Grady instead of Frances Netto.

Two hours later, I pouted my lips in front of my bathroom mirror while applying a thick swipe of my favorite red lipstick. I had straightened my curly hair for the holiday party and the ends now reached mid-way down my back. I barely recognized myself in the long, straight hair, heavy makeup, and tight red dress. I hoped no one from the mailroom would recognize me either. I would avoid them, anyway.

"Whoa! Where are you going looking like that?" asked Marco, walking past the bathroom door.

"Office party," I said, spraying a humidity blocker on my hair.

"Well, make sure you give your boss a big kiss from me."

I stopped spraying and turned to Marco. "What?"

"You know, for giving you an advance on your paycheck so you can help me pay for college." I cringed and he saw it. "You are still getting that advance? It's okay if they changed their mind. I'll—"

"No, no. It's just that not many people know about it. So, let's just keep it between us. Wouldn't want everyone asking for an advance."

"Yeah. Sure thing. Have fun tonight, Frannie."

"Thanks, Marco."

"You deserve it."

My eyes watered and I put down the bottle on the bathroom counter to hug him. "You deserve to be happy too," I whispered.

"Of course I do," he chuckled. "Now, get out of here. I need to go to the bathroom."

"Ugh, gross." I picked up my lipstick and went back to my room.

I grabbed the nude high heels Erika had lent me, the ones with the red soles, and rushed down the stairs. My parents were both at work and *Nonna* was kneading dough in the kitchen.

"Making cookies again?" I asked.

"Only a few dozen for Christmas. San Martini cookies are your father's favorite."

The sweet fig cookie was indeed my dad's favorite. And despite my grandmother being my mom's mother, she always remembered to make my dad's favorite dessert around the holidays.

Turning toward me, my grandmother did a double-take. "Francesca! You look beautiful!"

"Thank you, *Nonna*," I said and bussed a kiss on her cheek.

"You remind me of when I was your age," she said. "All the boys in the village wanted to sit behind my family at church."

I snatched my purse from the closet. "Well, I'm not looking for any attention tonight."

"You could have fooled me," she said with a chuckle.

Standing in the hallway, I watched my grandmother as she continued to punch flour into her mixture. Was she right? Was I trying to attract attention? Not really. I was trying to look like somebody other than Frances tonight. Maybe if a certain CEO noticed, what was the harm in that? It would all be over next week.

***

"Holy smokes, Frannie! Why have you been hiding underneath those baggy sweaters all these years?" Erika grabbed me as soon as I stepped off the elevator onto the twelfth floor. Garland framed all the doorways, trimmed with red holly. An eight-foot-tall Christmas tree stood where the couches in the reception area used to be and the smell of cinnamon and brown sugar permeated the air.

"Wow, the social committee outdid themselves this year," I said, looking at a table with Santa hats and jingle bells. There was even a real-life Santa sitting in a red chair taking pictures with the staff.

"Who's that?" I asked Erika.

"Clive! He finally got his butt up to the twelfth floor."

We both started giggling, and Erika wrapped her arm over my shoulder to hold me up so we wouldn't fall over. My gaze caught a pair of green eyes staring at me. He held a drink in his hand and was speaking to his brother Ryan, but his eyes followed my every move. I straightened my legs and pushed my hair off my shoulder.

"I see Colton is here already," I whispered.

Erika rolled her eyes. "All he's done is stare at those elevator doors." Looking at him, she continued. "He also scowls at anyone that speaks to him. Ryan's the only one wanting to get close to him so far. I can confidently say we're all happy you're here, Frannie."

"Me? Why would I have anything to do with his mood?"

"Oh, please. Ever since you started working as his assistant, he hasn't yelled or glared at anyone. If I wasn't worried about you getting caught, I'd ask you to stay on forever."

"Oh, don't be ridiculous." I had nothing to do with Colton's mood swings. To think otherwise would be trouble. No, he was just a moody man. Noticing Erika's ensemble, I smiled. "I like your dress and, wow, that headband is incredible." It was green with a string of holly running through it. "Where did you get it?"

"I made it myself," she said, grinning from ear to ear. "I'm thinking of starting a little side hustle. Maybe you can help me with the business plan."

"Would love to. I want to repay you for everything you've done for me. I can't thank you enough for the dress and shoes," I said, pulling down on the hem of the tight dress.

"I knew it would look good on you. I didn't know you'd walk in here looking like Helen of Troy." She laughed.

Her compliment raised my confidence. "I wanted to look different. Be sure no one mistook me for Frannie."

"The only person people are going to mistake you for is Colton's girlfriend if he doesn't stop staring at you like that. He looks about ready to scoop you up and carry you over his shoulder like some caveman."

I snuck a glance at Colton. He was indeed still staring at me. His brother was talking to someone else next to him, and while Colton was close, he might as well have been a thousand miles away. He didn't even pretend to be listening to their conversation. He sipped his drink and watched me.

A zing of power raced through me at that moment. I held the attention of the most ruthless man in the room. Someone who could take over corporations with less thought than most people put into choosing their clothes for the day. He intimidated almost everyone in this office, including me. But right now, I felt like I held his attention in the palm of my hand.

I must have stared back for too long. "He's coming over here," I whispered to Erika.

"Oh, lord," Erika groaned just before we both turned to face his approach.

"Ladies, thank you both for coming this evening. The social committee has done a spectacular job."

Erika's mouth fell open, so I jumped in.

"Yes. They really have. It's better than—"

Erika pressed her foot over mine. "It's better than anything I've seen before," I said before I could tell him it was better than last year's.

"Can I get you anything to drink?" he asked.

Erika held up her glass. "I'm good. But thanks."

"Ava?"

"Sure. That would be great. Thank you."

When he walked away, Erika pulled me aside. "That was close, Frannie."

"I know." I blew out a breath. "I just can't think straight when he's around."

"Maybe you should just quit before you say something and he realizes the truth."

"I can't. Not yet. I've made it through the first five days. I can do another five."

"I hope you're right."

I smoothed out the creases I knew were certainly on my face and pasted on a smile by the time Colton returned with my drink. "Here you go," he said, handing me a glass of eggnog.

"Thanks," I said and took a sip.

Still watching me, he asked, "Care to take a photo with Santa?"

I watched as people lined up to take a picture with Clive and knew he probably wouldn't recognize me, but I didn't want to tempt fate.

"I'd rather not," I said. Then, noticing a group from the mailroom walk toward us, I added, "How about we take a photo in the photo booth instead?"

I grabbed his hand and pulled him away from my downstairs

colleagues. He stared at our clasped hands and I immediately let go. "I'm sorry," I said.

"Don't be," he whispered and interlaced his fingers with mine.

Oh, god! Why did that feel so good and so right?

He sat down in the photo booth first and kept his legs wide open in typical male fashion. He patted his thigh and I laughed.

"If I didn't sit on Santa's lap, what makes you think I'd sit on yours?"

"I'm hoping it's because you want to. And despite being prim and proper, I'm praying that you want to be bad right now."

My breath hitched. I did want to sit on his lap. I wanted to straddle it, actually. But I hadn't realized it was written all over my face. I couldn't do it, though. It would be too intimate and I knew I would lose more than my job. I could easily lose my heart to this man.

"We really shouldn't," I said. "I'll just sit right here."

I tapped his knee with my own, forcing him to make space on the seat for me. He pressed the countdown button and wrapped his arm over my shoulder.

Click!

Oh boy! I knew his one-arm hug would look suspicious to anyone glancing at the picture. It would look like we were a couple. I should do something silly, something that wouldn't seem too intimate. I turned to face him and stuck out my tongue. Except, he turned, at the same time, and my tongue pressed against his bottom lip.

Click!

Oh no! That was bad. So very bad. Colton's eyes bore into mine and the fire behind them nearly burnt me. Then he placed both hands on either side of my cheeks and pulled my face to his.

Click!

Oh, forget it. I melted in his arms and kissed him back. I released all the tension I held in my shoulders this past week from lying to him, and finally allowed honesty to pour out of my mouth. The truth was that I wanted him. I couldn't deny it any longer. But I couldn't have him. Not as Ava and definitely not as Frannie. But as the lady in red at the office party, maybe, just maybe, I could have him for a minute. I sucked on his bottom lip and moaned into his mouth. He moved one hand through my hair to grab the back of my head, while the other pulled me closer from the waist. A harsh breath escaped his lips for a moment and he breathed out, "Ava."

Another woman's name on his lips, at a moment when I gave myself to him, destroyed me. So, I pulled away.

"We should get the pictures before anyone else sees them," I said, and pulled back the curtain to the photo booth.

The booth printed the photo and I tore it from the machine. My stomach sank as I looked at our faces. Desire, impatience, hunger. It was all there. But so was the chasm of my lie. He wasn't kissing Frances Netto. He thought he was kissing Ava Grady. My eyes watered and I walked away.

"Ava," Colton called, but I ignored him. I knew that if he looked into my eyes at that moment, he'd see the truth. That I was a fake.

"Hey, darling!" A hand reached out and squeezed my shoulder. "I don't think you've taken a picture with Santa yet."

I didn't turn around, but I knew the voice belonged to Clive. My back stiffened. *Oh, no!* If Clive looked directly at me, he would certainly recognize me. I closed my eyes and prepared to ignore him when another voice boomed from behind. "Get your hands off of her!"

Oh great! This was far worse. Clive yanked his hand back and stammered, "Yes, sir. Of course."

Humiliated, I ran down the hallway and into the washroom. Grabbing the sink with both hands, I dropped my head and panted. I tried to steady my breaths, but it was no use.

Oh, god! What did I do? I've brought the entire office's attention to myself. Now everyone must think something's going on between Colton and me.

A knock sounded at the door and it opened slowly. I knew it was him, even before his brown Italian leather shoes appeared next to the sink.

"Are you all right?" he asked.

I nodded. "Fine, thank you."

"Ava,"

"Please," I begged. I couldn't bear to hear that name on his lips right now. "I can't do this."

"Do what?" he asked, taking a step closer.

"Pretend anymore," I cried, and let out the sob I'd held back for so long.

"Ah, *sweetheart*," he said, putting his arm around me. I turned toward him, and he lifted my chin with his finger. "I don't want to pretend anymore, either."

I didn't get a chance to ask him what he meant because he brushed my hair back and devoured my mouth before I could even form the words. Emotion took over reason and I needed to feel cared for right now more than anything else. I cupped the back of his head and held on as tightly as I could. Moving his mouth to my ear, he whispered. "Come with me." He opened the washroom door and reached back to grab my hand.

"I'm not ready to face them," I said.

"You have nothing to be embarrassed about. I'm the one who caused the scene. But we can go back to my office if you prefer."

I nodded and followed him out the door. Fortunately, the hallway from the washroom to his office was away from the party, and no one saw us enter.

He pulled me back into his arms and kissed me. Then walked me toward the back of his office without breaking contact. I hadn't noticed where he'd brought me until my heels clicked on porcelain tiles. I looked around while Colton shut the door.

"A bathroom?" I asked, taking in the large en suite. A thought popped up in my head. "This is where you were when I walked into your office that day. I wondered where you had come from."

"It's the only place I can guarantee our privacy," he said, pushing my hair back. "You look incredible." His eyes roamed down my body.

My lungs felt tight, as though I couldn't breathe. I'd dreamt of him saying something like this to me for years, and now that he did, I didn't know how to respond. So, I wet my lips, preparing to say something sexy. "Thank you," was all that came to mind. *Come on, Frances!*

"I tried to resist you," he continued. "I really did. But when I held you and kissed you in that photo booth, something inside me snapped."

This couldn't be happening. This couldn't be Colton saying these words to me now. My heart raced and my mind went blank.

"Tell me you feel it too," he said.

I felt it long before today. "Yes," I whispered, staring up at him. His eyes heated and he took my mouth again as he grabbed me by the waist and lifted me onto the white marble countertop.

My skin tingled as he ran his hands up my dress and tightened his fingers on the back of my thighs. "Your skin is cold," he said.

I closed my eyes, reveling in his touch. "I don't feel cold."

Bringing his lips next to my ear, he growled, "Let's see if you can feel this."

He dropped to his knees and placed a kiss on the inside of my thigh. The heat from his lips sizzled up my leg and shot straight to my core. He ran his tongue in the same direction. My body hummed under his touch, but I stopped him.

"We can't," I said, my hand shaking as I pushed against his

shoulder, stopping him from advancing to the one place I wanted his lips the most.

"Why not?" he asked, his voice muffled next to my sensitive skin.

"Because..." I stammered. I wanted to shout, because you're not kissing Ava, you're kissing Frances. Instead, I whispered, "Because you're my boss."

He pulled his head back and raised himself to stare into my eyes. He held me there, his eyes searching mine.

"You're right, I'm the boss. So, I need no one's permission... but yours. You're the only one who can put an end to this right now. The power is all in your hands." His own trembled at my thighs as he spoke.

I swallowed.

"Do you want me?" he asked.

"Yes," I breathed out. I couldn't deny it. I couldn't lie about that. "But not here."

He nodded. "I understand." He stepped back only for a moment, then returned to face me. "But *woman*, I need you." He pulled me closer and pushed my hair back from my face so I would look up at him. "Come away with me this weekend, *sweetheart*."

My heart raced and my head shouted 'no'. But he hadn't called me Ava. That was my undoing.

"Yes," I whispered and closed my eyes, praying I hadn't just made the biggest mistake of my life.

6

Frances

I packed my face wash and moisturizer into my overnight bag. Spotting my eBook reader on the nightstand, I considered bringing it along but realized it probably wouldn't be necessary. *I'd be too busy to read.* My stomach clenched in anticipation and apprehension at the same time.

After zipping the bag, I dialed Erika's number.

"Hello?"

"Hey, it's me." I sat down on my bed, pushing my hair back from my forehead.

"Are you packed?" she asked in a stern voice. To say Erika was displeased with my weekend plans would be an understatement.

"Yep. You remember what we talked about?"

"Yes. I'll lie for you. If Marco or your parents call, I'll tell them you're with me."

"Thank you. I said something about visiting your family in Chicago."

"I don't have family in Chicago."

"I know that, but they don't."

Her harsh breath crackled over the phone. "You know, lying is usually a good indication that you're doing something you shouldn't be doing in the first place."

"Not in this case. I'm lying to help my brother."

"Sleeping with your boss won't help your brother, Frannie. So don't give me that."

My eyes watered. But I didn't have to worry about Erika seeing me, so I didn't wipe the tear that fell down my cheek. "You're right. I'm doing this for me. For once in my life, I want to be selfish and do something just for myself. Not because it's the right thing to do, but because it's not."

She sighed. "You really should have rebelled more as a teenager, you know."

I should have done a lot more in college, too. But he'd said I didn't need any of that. All I needed was him. It sounded so romantic at the time. Now, the memory makes me want to throw up.

"Just be careful. Don't do anything you don't want to do. And if he hurts you, you call me and I'll mess him up."

I snorted but knew Erika wasn't kidding. She had my back and I had hers. It would always be that way between us. "I've got to go. Thank you and I love you."

"Love you too."

I grabbed my bag and raced down the stairs. Marco stood at the stove next to *Nonna*, scrambling eggs while she sprinkled icing sugar on the pancakes.

"That looks delicious," I said.

"It tastes even better," said Marco, flashing me a grin. "Sit down, eggs are almost ready."

"I can't." I slung the bag's strap over my shoulder. "I have a plane to catch. I'll see you both Sunday night."

"Have fun," he called out while spooning the eggs onto a plate. "Say hello to Erika for me. And don't forget to put in a good word. I'm nearly a college boy now."

He chuckled, and *Nonna* smacked his shoulder.

"Sorry, kid," I teased. "Still not man enough for Erika."

"What! *Nonna*, did you hear that?" He raised the spoon, causing some eggs to fall onto the floor.

"Marco, you're making a mess everywhere," she yelled. Then to me, "Be careful, Francesca."

"I will, *Nonna*," I said and closed the door behind me.

A black sedan sat in my driveway, and for a minute, I thought he'd gotten the wrong house. Until the driver, dressed in a black suit and tie, stepped out and asked for me by name. Or rather, Ava. I was starting to really dislike her.

"Yes, that's me," I said and cautiously looked over my shoulder to ensure no one was watching through the window. Thank goodness they were both busy in the kitchen.

The driver walked up and grabbed the bag from my shoulder, then opened the backseat door and waved me inside. It was nice and warm inside the vehicle. Despite the sunny sky, it was still chilly outside.

Having thrown out my resume, Colton had asked for my address to send a car to pick me up. I'd expected a ride-sharing service, not this fancy car. I was glad he hadn't come himself, though.

Earlier, Marco had insisted on driving us but I'd said that Erika and I were taking a taxi to the airport. So, if he saw the fancy driver outside, he'd know something else was up.

"I don't mean to be rude, but can we get going? I'm in a bit of a rush."

"Don't worry, Ms. Grady. I'll get you to the airport in plenty of time." He pulled out of the driveway and I inhaled deeply. It wasn't the plane I was worried about.

True to his word, we arrived at the airport in no time.

"Um. You missed the Departures exit," I said, pointing to the sign overhead.

"Mr. Crawford is taking his private plane to Miami, ma'am. The runway is this way."

Private plane? Miami? He'd said we wouldn't be traveling far, but I had thought maybe we were headed to New York or Boston for the weekend. Not Florida! Thank goodness I'd packed a bathing suit, prepared for a hot tub or something. Or something was right.

My purse vibrated next to me. I pulled out my phone and saw an incoming call from the store I'd interviewed at earlier. I didn't want to speak to the owner, Marcus, right now. Not with the driver listening. I would call him back when I returned from Miami.

As the driver pulled up next to a small plane, Colton descended the stairs. At first, only his blue jeans were visible, but then a broad chest inside a fitted black sweater came into view. The aviator sunglasses nearly did me in. He was gorgeous and I couldn't stop a sigh from my lips.

The driver opened my door and I stepped out of the car. Colton was there in two strides. Pulling the sunglasses off of his face, he smiled and tiny creases formed next to his eyes. "Hi," he said and leaned down to kiss my cheek.

I smiled. "Hi."

He interlaced his fingers with mine and pulled me toward the plane. "I'm sorry I could not pick you up myself. I needed to check on a few things before departure. Was the ride all right?"

"Yes, it was perfect," I said. "Are we really going to Miami?"

"Ah, so Eric ruined the surprise," he grinned. "Yes. Have you ever been?"

"No. Never."

"Well, I'm happy to ease you into your first trip to the sunshine state. Or not, if you prefer I don't go gently."

I blushed and he laughed. "You know, for someone in complete control at work, you are easy to tease when it comes to sex."

I sucked in my lips. He had noticed. I was trying, I really was.

"After you, Ms. Grady," he said and placed his hand on my lower back to take the first step onto the plane.

I held onto the railing and raised my foot. My leg shook, but I breathed through my nose, steadying my heartbeat.

You can do this! He likes you and you like him. You're doing nothing wrong.

An attendant met me at the top of the stairs. "Good morning!"

"Morning," I said, and walked into the cabin furnished with white leather seats and black trim. Four seats faced each other on the left, while a long couch and table protruded on the right. A closed door in the center.

Colton's hand on my shoulder shook me from my state of shock, and I walked over to one of the seats. "I assume it's your first time on a private plane, too."

I simply nodded, still unable to speak.

What the heck was I doing here? I was lying to someone that could probably kill me and hide all the evidence without lifting a finger.

That was unfair. Colton wasn't a criminal. Yet, I've seen him flip out when someone puts him on hold for too long. My heart hammered in my chest and my throat felt tight.

"Are you all right?" asked Colton when I sucked in a breath and nearly choked on air.

"Yes," I said, cupping both hands over my mouth to steady my breathing. *You are overreacting, Frances. Calm down.*

"Are you nervous about flying?"

"I don't know. I've never flown in a private plane before."

"Would you like something to take the edge off?"

"Like what?"

"Why don't we start with a glass of wine?"

I nodded. Wine sounded freaking fantastic. I unzipped my coat and placed it on the couch.

Colton poured a glass of white wine for me as I rubbed my

hands together. I suddenly felt cold. Maybe it was nerves. I breathed in the tangy smell and closed my eyes when the sweetness exploded on my tongue.

Yes, this is much better.

"Thank you," I said when he sat down next to me. "Aren't you going to pour one for yourself?"

"Nah. I want nothing on my tongue except for you."

I spewed the drink across the floor and onto the table. "Oh my god! I'm so sorry," I said, grabbing a napkin from the table and wiping down the mess. The flight attendant scurried over and I swear I heard her tsk under her breath. Regardless, the look she gave me was disapproving enough.

Colton, on the other hand, laughed so hard he pressed a fist to his mouth.

"You did that on purpose," I whispered harshly.

"I didn't. I swear," he said between breaths. "But I can't promise I won't in the future."

His boyish grin ripped off the last of my defenses, and I sunk into my chair. He leaned over me and said, "I don't mind that you made a mess of the cabin, but next time, try to swallow." He stared down at my lips and I watched him as he moved inch by excruciating inch closer to me until he finally pressed his lips against mine. His tongue swept the inside of my mouth and his hand pressed down on the headrest, sinking me further into my seat.

"I want you so bad, Ava."

My head spun, and my heart hammered against my chest. Colton made me feel alive and terrified at the same time. I didn't know what to do about it. "Colton," I said. "I need to take it slow."

He closed his eyes and swore harshly under his breath. "I'm so sorry. You're right. I'm all over you like some teenage boy."

He sat back in his seat next to me and ran his hand through his hair. "You set the pace. I'll take my cues from you."

Being in control again felt like someone turned a jackhammer off. Inhaling a quick breath, I turned to the side to look at Colton. He sat with his eyes closed, his mouth in a straight line.

I leaned over. "Thank you," I whispered in his ear. Goosebumps raised along the side of his neck, and he squeezed the leather armrests, his knuckles turning as white as the leather.

"No problem," he ground out and I smiled. I felt heady from the power he gave to me, and I wanted to test my strength over him. I'd never felt that way before. I'd never been the one to set the pace, to decide the next move. My mind raced with seductive things I would say next, but I couldn't say any of them out loud.

"Colton," I said instead.

"Yes, *baby*?"

"You may not like the pace I set."

He smiled but kept his eyes closed. "As long as we're moving, *sweetheart*, I'll not complain."

7

Frances

Another car waited on the tarmac for us when the plane landed in Miami. This time, Colton opened the car door for me and I scooted in. He pressed the palm of his hand over mine and interlaced our fingers. The man didn't shy away from intimacy. I wasn't used to any kind of public display of affection.

We drove along the coast and I stared up at the palm trees, their branches swaying in the wind. The sun shined down into the car and I took off my coat, letting the sun hit my face and neck.

"Which hotel are we staying at?" I asked while putting on my sunglasses.

"We're not staying in one at all. I have a house here."

Of course he did. Private planes, fancy cars, multiple homes. The gap between Colton's life and the world I knew grew even further. It wasn't just my lie that kept us apart. Some days, it felt like we lived on different planets.

The car pulled up onto a gray interlock driveway lined with palm trees. The sprawling white stucco mansion must have been at least four times the size of my detached house. With two large balcony doors at the front, four garages on the side, and two front doors, I wasn't sure where to look for the entrance to the home.

Colton stepped out of the car first, and I pushed myself to follow, feeling more trepidation now that we were here. Walking up to the front steps, I stared at the steel double doors spanning the length of a car. Where would one even find doors like these?

Punching in a code on a keypad lock, Colton swung open the door. The breeze hit my face and the smell of the salty ocean encircled me. Smaller palm trees decorated the foyer, contrasting against the white walls. But the blue mosaic tile on the floor halted me. It was like walking on water. I hesitantly took a step forward and smiled when I didn't plunge in.

"This place is incredible, Colton," I said. He walked to the end of the foyer and opened the glass door, letting the sound of the waves crash in.

"So are you," he said, walking back to me. "You know, you're the first person I've ever brought here."

"I am? Why me?"

"Because you didn't know it existed."

Funny, he didn't know I existed either until I stood in his office. Even then, he thought I was someone else.

"What would you like to do?" he asked.

"I'm not sure. I've never been to Miami."

"Well, what do you like to do in general?" He raised his hand and slid his finger along the side of my face.

"Um. I like to read," I stammered.

"What else?"

"I don't know." I was hesitant to divulge too much of my personal life, but I thought maybe this would be safe. "When I'm home, I usually play cards with my brother and grandmother."

He smiled. "You play cards?"

"I know. It sounds lame saying it out loud. But my grandmother gets so angry when she loses, it's quite funny."

"I don't think it's lame at all. I've got an idea."

I tilted my head. "You want to play Uno or something?" I teased.

He smiled. "Not exactly. Why don't you change for dinner? Then I'll take you somewhere I think you'll like."

My stomach did a tiny flip. The mysterious way he planned our date excited me. I hadn't liked surprises in a long time. But for some inexplicable reason, I trusted Colton.

"All right. Just give me fifteen minutes."

He leaned down and kissed my lips. "I'll be right here waiting."

I scurried halfway up the stairs and turned. "Where do I go? I might get lost in this place."

He chuckled and walked with me the rest of the way up and through the hallway. He turned into a bedroom with hardwood floors, a fireplace, and a four-post bed in the center. "The bathroom is just over there," he said, pointing to a door to the left. Then he closed the bedroom door behind him.

I unzipped my bag and pulled out a black wrap dress I'd brought and my wedge sandals. I freshened up in the bathroom and changed as quickly as I could. Touching up my makeup and spraying down my hair, I readied myself faster than I ever had before. Adrenaline pumped in my veins and my hands shook.

Is this excitement or nerves? Maybe a bit of both.

After applying some red lipstick, I snuck one last look in the mirror and nodded.

You got this, Frances. Don't be scared.

Sitting on a bench in the foyer, distracted by his phone, Colton didn't see me walk down the stairs.

"Hi," I said when I reached the last step.

He swung his head toward me. "Hey—" He seemed to stop mid-sentence and run his hand over his lips. "Wow. You look amazing."

I wanted to point to the dress and say 'this old thing' but knew it was too close to the truth to be funny. So, I thanked him instead.

"Are you going to tell me where we're headed?"

He held my hand as we walked toward a red sports car parked out front. "Not yet," he said, opening my car door.

When he sat inside, he turned to look at me and bit his lip. "You're dangerous, you know that? I may go to jail tonight for beating the guys off of you."

I laughed and shook my head. "That's one of the worst lines I've ever heard."

"All right, Ms. Grady. I will work to improve my game. Now, let's see if you've got any."

He pulled out of the circular driveway and onto the road. I watched the homes we drove past through the passenger window and imagined what it would be like to live in something so big and luxurious. Did the people inside even realize what they had? Did they appreciate it? Or were they thinking of their next purchase?

A few minutes later, Colton pulled onto a dark road, and fear reared its familiar head. "Where are we?" I asked, my fingers splayed on my chest. I reached for my neck, wanting to pull down my collar to help me breathe, but there was nothing there strangling me except for my own thoughts.

"Colton?" I whispered, staring at the dark forest and darkened pathway. When he didn't respond and the road didn't lighten, I panicked.

I was transported to a memory from my past to a place I never wished to return to again. It was dark and cramped and I was scared. I screamed his name, over and over again, but he never came. No one did. Not for a very long time.

"Colton, turn around. I want to go back. Where are you taking me?" I shouted.

"Hey," he soothed, reaching for my hand that now tore at the skin on my neck. I couldn't breathe.

"Ava. What's wrong?" he asked, bringing my hand on top of his thigh.

A tiny light glimmered ahead, and my chest loosened. "We're here," he said, pulling up to the top of the road. Bright lights illuminated an enormous parking lot. So many lights now that I squinted. I read the blinking sign: CASINO.

After parking the car, Colton turned off the engine but didn't get out. Instead, he faced me and held my hand. "What happened back there?" His brow furrowed as he waited.

I swallowed. Humiliated and still a little scared, tears brimmed my eyes, but I held them back. "I'm sorry."

"Don't apologize," he said, staring at my face. His intense look prodded at my armor, but it was still well in place. "Do you want to turn back?"

"No." I shook my head. "It was silly. Sometimes dark places trigger me. I'm fine," I said, sounding the opposite of fine.

"Are you sure?"

"Yes." I squeezed his hand and opened my car door. I couldn't stand being in the closed car any longer. He led me toward the entrance, wrapping an arm around my shoulder. I closed my eyes and allowed his warmth to comfort me. I smiled. I didn't know how much I needed someone's gentle touch until it was on me. Wrapping my arm around his waist, I squeezed my thanks.

He pulled open the glass front door and immediately the sound of machines ringing and voices shouting surrounded us. Hundreds of people gathered in one large room. It reminded me of a giant arcade, but with better lighting and staff walking around with free sodas and water.

"Where should we start? Do you like cards, dice, or slots?" asked Colton.

"Um. Not sure. I've only ever played the slot machines before."

"Well, let's make this weekend about us discovering new things. Shall we?" He walked me through the narrow rows of slot machines.

"Since it's your first time, I'll go easy on you," he whispered in my ear, and goosebumps formed along my arms.

"You don't have to curb your pleasure on my account," I told him, afraid I was holding him back.

"*Sweetheart*, my pleasure is all based on your account," he whispered.

Colton's words zipped through my body and lit me up like these damn slot machines.

Pointing to a large crowd, I asked, "What's that?" The crowd immediately groaned and some threw their hands up in the air.

"Let's find out." He led me toward them, and I wormed my way through a small space to take a peek. A large gaming table had everyone's attention. A man stood at the top and threw a pair of dice. The crowd groaned again. "Maybe it's time to change the energy," said Colton, pushing my hair off my shoulder. "Do you want to place a bet?"

I shook my head. "I've no idea what I'm doing in this game."

"Often, that's the best time to play. Beginner's luck and all."

I looked at the faces of those around me. I'd no desire to make them groan again because of something I'd rolled. "Maybe something less communal and more one-on-one."

"Ah, I think I've got it." He led me away from the large craps table and toward a smaller, semi-circular one.

"Have you ever played Black Jack?"

"No. But I know how it's played."

"Great. Take a seat."

"Colton, no. I couldn't. I didn't even bring cash."

He smiled and dropped a fifty on the table. "You can pay me back later," he said.

"What if I mess everyone up?"

"I'll take the seat at the end, the anchorman position. That's the only one anyone remarks upon. You'll be safe beside me." I believed him.

"It's a cold deck," said a player to the right of me. Having no idea what it meant, I replied. "Then let's hope it warms up."

He smiled and turned to the dealer. "Let her cut the cards."

The dealer hands me a card and signals to the deck. I turned to Colton, ready to bail. He placed his hand on my fingers and said, "Just place the card anywhere in the deck."

I nodded and moved my hand to cut the cards. "I would have brought it up closer," said Colton in a low voice.

"What?" I shrieked.

He laughed and rubbed my thigh. "Relax. I'm just messing with you."

"Not funny, Colton."

His smile dropped and his eyes heated. "God. I didn't know I had a kink for you saying my name."

I blushed and turned over my card. It was a two. The card showing on the table was a king. I scanned the other cards on the table. Threes, fours, and sixes.

The first player at our table asked for a card. It was a seven. "Hit me again," said the player. This time the dealer turned over a three. "I'll stand."

The player next to me had a similar run.

I peeked at my card again. I only had twelve in total. I needed twenty-one, but so far no other face cards except for my king had come out. If I asked for a card and it was a king, queen, or jack, it would be game over for me. That much I knew.

"I'll stay," I said.

Colton raised his eyebrow. "Are you sure?"

I nodded and looked down at his card. He showed a six on the table.

"All right," he said, then to the dealer, "Hit me."

The dealer turned over the next card. Queen of Spades. "Damn it," cursed Colton, and turned over his hand. He held the Jack of Diamonds.

"You should have held on sixteen, dude," said the man beside me.

"Thanks for your advice," mumbled Colton. But that was it. He didn't threaten the man. He didn't call him out or call him names. For having the reputation of a jerk, sometimes Colton surprised me with his control.

The dealer turned over a card for himself, and it was a king. That gave him sixteen and beat my twelve. I sighed. "That sucks. I lost."

"Hold on," said Colton. "The dealer can't stand on sixteen. He must hit."

I squeezed my free hand into a fist and waited. The next card the dealer turned over was the Jack of Hearts.

"Yes," cried the man beside me.

"I won?" I asked, turning to Colton. He wrapped his arm around my waist and kissed my cheek.

"You won, *sweetheart*!" he said.

I threw my arms around his neck and squeezed. "I won! I won my first hand!" He held me tightly in his arms. When I pulled away, I wondered aloud, "Beginner's luck, I guess."

"Nah. You didn't just get lucky. You were smart about it." Then he kissed me softly. "But maybe I'll get lucky later."

I bit my lip, hiding my smile, and turned back to the dealer. "Let's go again."

I won the next five hands. The guy next to me high-fived me, and Colton exclaimed, "That's my girl," at least twice.

I won six hundred dollars that night. It would have been more, but I was too scared to double down when Colton suggested it.

"This is the most money I've ever held in my hands," I said, staring down at the bills.

"What do you plan to buy yourself with your earnings?" he asked, grabbing my free hand and lacing our fingers together.

Without hesitation, I responded, "Books!"

"Quite the bookworm, I see."

"Not for me," I clarified. "For my brother. He starts college in the spring. He was going to read them online, but now I can buy him ones he can highlight!"

He stared at me and shook his head. "You're amazing."

I smirked. "I'm a pretty awesome sister, I know."

"Ready to eat?" asked Colton when we got to the car.

"Definitely."

"Do you mind if we dine at home? I don't think I can share you with a room full of people any longer."

Home. Funny how that one word made me feel so warm inside. "That sounds wonderful."

8

Colton

Ava was the real deal. She wasn't fake and didn't worry about laughing too loudly or drinking regular soda. I was really starting to like her. *Shit.*

When she said she planned to spend her winnings to buy books for her brother, I nearly dropped to one knee and proposed. I mean, I didn't even want to get married and she had me thinking these thoughts.

As I drove us back to the house, I turned to look at her while at a traffic light. She sat staring out her window, winding a curl of brown hair around her finger. I felt just like that strand of hair wrapped around her flesh. She twisted my insides and made me want to say things I had never imagined saying. Like "back home". *Where did that come from?* Why didn't I just say back to my place?

After reaching the house, I turned off the engine and shifted my body to face her. There was something about this woman that constantly drew me to her. I pulled the curl away from her hand and kissed her fingers. Despite the warmer climate, they were cold. "Let's go inside," I said.

After she climbed out of the car, I held her close to me and rubbed her bare arm. She had goosebumps on her flesh and I wanted to erase them from her body. "Is everything all right?"

"Yes," she said, biting her lip. She seemed nervous.

"Do you like sushi?" I asked, unlocking the front door.

"I do."

"Great. Make yourself comfortable."

She removed her sandals and walked barefoot on the blue porcelain floors. With her long hair flowing halfway down her back and the sexy sway of her hips, she reminded me of some ocean goddess sent here to tempt me.

I removed a tray of sushi from the fridge. My staff always stocked the fridge and sushi was one of my staples. Grabbing the spicy mayo and wasabi, I carried the tray to the dining room. Ava joined me.

"I love the view from here," she said, standing in front of the double French doors.

"It's incredible." My voice dropped as I admired her silhouette against the backdrop of the sunset. "Why don't we eat outside?"

Her brilliant smile suggested the idea appealed to her. As I opened the French doors, the smell of the salty ocean surrounded me. I set the tray down on a small white coffee table next to the gray and white daybed. I arranged the pillows so we could sit up comfortably.

"After you," I said, pointing to the pillows.

She slid onto the daybed and stretched out her legs. I sat next to her and reached for her hand as we both stared out at the soothing scenery. The backyard faced west. There were no obstructions; nothing between us and the sunset. It was perfect.

"This seems unreal," she said, snuggling into my side. I followed her gaze as she watched the path of a bird in flight. Turning my head to stare at her, I agreed. "It sure does." I couldn't stop staring at her full mouth. "But it's better than anything I could have imagined."

She turned to look at me and smiled, her cheeks rounding into tempting peaches. I wanted to know if they were as soft as they looked, so I ran my thumb across her face. Her smooth skin felt like velvet across my rough hands.

"Shall we dig in?" she asked, looking down at the tray with one shoulder raised and wet her lips.

Catching a glimpse of her tongue, I groaned inwardly. Needing a distraction, I picked up the tray on the table by the daybed, hoping the food would take my mind off of her sweet mouth. "Ladies first."

She picked up a vegetable roll with a pair of chopsticks and took a bite. "Mmm. This is really good."

I popped a dynamite roll in my mouth and savored the taste of crab, avocado, shrimp, and cucumber. "It's not bad. Not as good as the place down the street from the office."

"Really? I've never been there." She took another piece.

"I'll have to take you when we get back," I said, realizing I was making plans with her for the future.

"Sushi is definitely a treat. My grandmother won't eat it so we never order it at home."

"Has she ever tried it?"

"Nope," she said with a smile. "Marco says she doesn't trust anything that isn't overcooked," she chuckled this time. "But he's always competing with her as the chef in the family."

Her happiness was palatable. "You're close to your family."

"I am," she said, taking a piece of the ginger and placing it on top of her next piece. "How about you? I've seen your brother Ryan a few times. Do you have any other siblings?"

"Yes. I have another brother named Luke. He's the baby, but no one better tell him that." I couldn't stop my grin. I loved talking about my brothers.

"What about your parents? Do they live in the area?" she asked.

I never spoke of my parents. Ever. It wasn't anyone's business what happened in the past and my chest tightened every time I thought of them. But this time, I was tempted to tell Ava more and share a piece of them with her. But I couldn't get the words through my lips. My usual prepared lines won over. "My parents died when we were young. Lived with foster parents until I was eighteen and then I moved me and my brothers out. Been just the three of us ever since."

"I'm sorry, Colton. I didn't know." Her eyes pierced mine and I felt them dive into my soul, searching for more.

"It was a long time ago. But it's still difficult for me to talk about."

"I understand," she said, nodding. Her eyes still held mine. "Sometimes there are things in our past that are too difficult to express into words."

I realized she wasn't just speaking about my experience. Based on her reaction in the car, she was hiding some darkness in her past. As much as I wanted to know, wanted to help her, I was afraid she'd expect me to reciprocate. So, I ended the conversation as best I could.

"Once I moved my brothers out, we moved on, and I haven't looked back since." *Liar.*

I looked back every single day, and I always would until I found the remaining pieces of my mother's jewelry. Then I could rest. Then I could forgive myself.

Those deep brown eyes did not let go, but her lips curved upwards a bit. "Don't take this the wrong way, but I thought you were some rich, trust fund baby who inherited daddy's money."

I smiled. "I am."

She covered her mouth. "Oh, god. I'm sorry I said that."

She was adorable when she blushed. It reminded me of sitting in front of a warm fire. I pulled her closer and leaned us back onto the pillows. "My dad owned his own company. After my parents passed away, my father's lawyer put our shares in trust until I became of age. I took the money and started Crawford Corp. It wasn't a fortune, but I would never have amassed the capital to start the company without it."

"I don't think that's the same thing as being a trust fund baby," she said.

"We had to work to get to where we are now, but when my parents were alive, we never wanted for anything."

"How old were you when they died?"

"Nine."

"That's so young." The concern in her voice tore at the wall that I'd built to protect the secrets of my past.

"Ryan was seven and Luke was five."

"You were lucky to have foster parents to raise you."

My jaw tightened, and my fist clenched. The wall came up again. "They were compensated," was all I could spit out.

She nodded but didn't press me further. I exhaled through my nostrils and changed the subject. "What's your family like?"

"They're overbearing," she said with a snort and covered it with her hand. "But I love them. My parents never let us go to bed angry, never let Marco and I argue and not make up. I hated it when I was a kid, but it helped us form a close bond." She played with a string on the pillow. Then softly, she added, "I would do anything for my brother."

"Do you ever think of getting your own place?"

She rolled her eyes. "All the time. But I can't afford the rent right now nor the living expenses. I've got a five-year plan, though."

"Your boss must be a real a-hole. You should ask him for a raise."

"Maybe I will," she said and nudged me with her knee.

She lowered her head, shying away, and her hair fell in front of her face. It bothered me that I couldn't see it anymore. Pushing her hair back behind her ear, I kissed her softly on the temple. Then lower, next to her jaw. My lips had a mind of their own as the world around us and the past faded away. She made me want to forget everything.

I ran my lips down her neck and licked at her collarbone, sliding my tongue to the small dip in the center. She inhaled sharply as I waited for a sign from her on how far I could go.

She's supposed to set the pace, Colton.

I pulled away to give her space, but she threw her head back and grabbed my shoulders. *Yes*, I rejoiced in my head. Her floral perfume intoxicated me as I continued to explore her neck. Her skin felt like silk against my lips.

When I reached the tip of her breast through her dress, I swept my tongue over that, too. She gripped my head against her chest, burrowing her fingers in my hair, and I lost my mind.

With a soft groan, I pushed her down onto the daybed and scattered the pillows onto the floor. Grabbing her wrist, I pulled it up above her head, then did the same to the other arm, raising her breasts high where I could taste them. *Mmm.*

She let out a whimper and I smiled at her response. Then her body tensed, like a corpse beneath me, and I raised my head to look into her eyes. They were closed, and her lips were sucked all the way into her mouth.

"Ava, *sweetheart*. What's wrong?"

She shook her head and I let go of her hands. I lifted myself off of her, but never took my eyes away from her pale face. It was smooth now, still like the ocean in front of us. When she opened her eyes, the distant look I saw in them cut through my chest.

"I don't like being held down," she said in a soft voice.

I nodded. Someone hurt her and I wanted, for the second time in my life, to commit murder. "Who did this to you?" I asked.

She shook her head, staring down at her hands. "It doesn't matter."

"It does to me," I said, feeling the words rumble in my chest.

She turned her body toward me. Her eyes roamed over my face, as though she searched for something hidden behind my words. But I'd meant every one of them. Slowly, she raised her hand and moved her thumb back and forth on my cheek. Something ignited between us, more than passion, more than lust. I didn't know what it was, but I knew it required more of me than what I'd been willing to give in past relationships.

Turning my face, I kissed the inside of her hand. How could anyone hurt her? "I'm sorry, Ava," I whispered. "I'm sorry I wasn't there to stop them."

"I'm all right." She gave me a weak smile. "It was a long time ago." Then, running her fingers down my cheek, she whispered, "Something about you makes me want more. That I deserve more."

"You deserve everything," I whispered. I inched closer to her face, pressing my lips softly to hers. "We can take it slowly," I said.

Her breathing was even now. "I haven't, well, I haven't done this in a long time," she said.

"We don't have to do anything," I assured her.

"Maybe if... maybe if I'm in control... I think... I would like that."

This time, I swallowed with difficulty. I saw the struggle in her eyes—the fight between want and worry—and I didn't know how to help her. So, I simply nodded.

She raised one knee over my body and sat down on my legs. My gaze fixed on her hands as she moved them over my shirt and across my chest. Despite the fabric, I reveled in every touch on my skin. She pulled at the hem, slowly bunching it up to my navel, and pressed her lips onto my stomach. Her mouth burned into my flesh as though she branded me wherever she kissed.

I held myself in place, bracing every muscle in my body, not wanting to move or scare her. My hands twitched to pull her down and hold her head against my lips, so I fisted them beside me instead. She stared at me, but I closed my eyes, fighting to control my desire when I saw the fire behind hers. Her delicate fingers unbuttoned my shirt and she ran her hands along my bare chest, stopping to brush against my nipples.

A shiver ran down my spine and along my legs. Her breath tickled my neck and I jerked when she sucked at the spot next to my shoulder. I'd never reacted this way to a simple kiss. "Can I touch you?" I whispered, my eyes still closed, praying she'd allow me this.

"Yes," she whispered next to my ear.

Slowly, my hands massaged her hips and just held her there.

"You asked to touch me, Colton. Is this the best you've got?"

My eyes flew open. A smile played on her lips and her eyes danced. She was so *fucking* beautiful. "*Sweetheart*, it would scare you to know how much I need you right now. I want to run my hands across every inch of your skin until your body's shaking and you're begging me to take you."

Desire raged in her eyes. She dropped her head and pushed her tongue through my lips, a groan vibrating through her. My hands flew to her face, down her neck, cupping her breasts. She lifted her head and licked her lips, lost in the moment.

Slowly, I pulled down her dress from the shoulders, revealing her bra. It was a flimsy lace thing and I raised my head to lick through it. She held my head there and I sucked at the puckered tip. The sounds she made drove me crazy, drowning out the ocean behind us. Wrapping my hands around her ass, I pushed her softness against me, offering me only momentary relief before the throbbing resumed. If she felt half the torture I did, I knew I had to do something. Raising the hem of her dress, I felt my way to the side of her panties. Those were lace, too. The intricate fabric never felt so damn good against my skin.

Pressing my thumb against her clit, she let out another whimper. "Are you all right?" I asked. She nodded but said nothing.

I continued, this time circling it with my thumb. Her mouth fell open and her eyes rolled back. She was close. Her breathing was harsh and she rocked against my thumb, needing more. Before I could increase the pressure, she fumbled with the button on my pants.

"Are you sure?" I asked, holding my breath.

"Yes," she panted. "But do you have protection?"

I reached for my wallet as she slowly unzipped my pants. Rolling on the condom, my desire for her intensified, and when I finally guided her body on top of mine, I groaned harshly from the pleasure of being inside of her. She was so warm and soft.

She squeezed me until I threw my head back onto the bed. Holding herself up on my shoulders, she rocked her body against me, rubbing and grinding.

Instinctively, my hands flew to her hips and I pushed down, pressing my fingers into her flesh. I realized what I'd done and loosened my hold. She didn't seem to notice, though, moving faster on top of me.

I pressed down on her clit again and her hands flew to her hair, lifting it off her shoulders. She brought them down behind her to hold on to my legs, arching her back. This beautiful woman riding me with the stars behind her was a vision I'd never forget.

I circled my thumb to her rhythm and she whimpered.

"Colton," she panted, and pleasure slammed into me from the sound of my name on her lips. "Yes!" she cried. Her legs stiffened, her fingers squeezed my thighs, and she fell forward.

Ah, yes.

I raised my hips off the bed and pushed deep inside of her. Burying myself to the hilt. I bit my lip to stop a shout, then came harder than I ever had before. *Holy Shit.*

That was unbelievable.

Her ragged breaths tickled my neck. Her body rose and fell with the rapid movements of my chest. I pulled her dress up onto her shoulders, covering her body, then wrapped my arms around her and squeezed. I never wanted to let her go.

9

Frances

"You did what?" Erika's eyes widened and her hands flew to her hips.

I knew she would be mad, but I had to tell someone about my weekend with Colton. I kept little from Erika. She even knew about *him*.

"It was wonderful," I said, doing a little pirouette in the middle of the twelfth-floor hallway while holding my morning cup of coffee. Colton was in a meeting and kept his office door closed.

"I'm glad you're happy. I really am, Frances," said Erika. "But you can't keep up the pretense forever. You're quitting at the end of this week and I don't want your heart broken."

Placing my coffee on her desk, I crossed my arms. "Why can't you just be happy for me?" Tears stung the back of my eyes, but I held them in check. Her words hurt because I couldn't disagree with them. "I just want to enjoy this for as long as I can. Is that too much to ask? To finally want something for me?"

She stood from the desk and wrapped her arms around me. "It's not too much to ask of me. But it may be too much to ask of yourself. I know you. You will be devastated if you let this get any further." A single tear escaped and I quickly wiped it away. "It may already be too late," she said and ran her finger across my cheek to catch the next one.

"Finally, I found someone who genuinely likes me and is kind to me," I said, straightening my spine and wiping my own tears.

"He thinks your name is Ava Grady. It's not real and you have to tell him before it goes any further."

Her aim was true, and her words struck my heart. He didn't make love to Frances Netto. He thought he had made love to Ava Grady. She was right. I'd already gone too far. I should take a step back and detach myself from Colton before I would have to leave for good in four days. But I couldn't.

"Just give me four days," I pleaded. "I deserve four days of happiness."

"You deserve way more than that. That's why I want you to end it now."

"I'll be fine. I promise."

Erika placed one hand back on her hip, and pointed a finger at me with the other. "You've got four days and then we're going out and getting drunk so you can forget about this whole mess."

I smiled, imagining Erika drunk and hitting on the bartender like she always did when she had one too many. But I also smiled to hide the thoughts gaining strength in my mind that I could never forget about Colton. "Deal," I said soberly and hugged her before walking back to my cubicle.

Colton's door was still closed, but his blinds were open. He paced his office, raising his voice for anyone on the twelfth floor to hear. When our eyes met, he stopped walking and waved me to come inside. I approached his desk as he scribbled on a yellow sticky note: Can you get me the Morgan file?

I nodded and left his office to retrieve the land registry and other paperwork in the Morgan file. I implemented a new filing system and found everything in seconds.

"What the heck is wrong with you?" Colton shouted into the phone. "How are we going to convince Morgan to sell us this property if we can't even get the project off the ground? You were supposed to get the mayor's office to approve these plans two days ago." He pounded his fist onto the desk and I flinched. I couldn't help it.

Colton's eyes shot to mine and I dropped the files next to the phone. I was about to leave and give him back his privacy when his hand covered mine on the desk. I stared at the tendons on his hands as his fingers curled over mine. When I raised my head, the concern in his eyes disarmed me. The tension in my shoulders eased and my heartbeat slowed down. I hadn't realized how much his outburst had scared me, but he'd noticed.

He caressed my hand with his thumb, and that simple movement was enough to melt my heart. I loved this man. I loved this irritable, smart, sexy man. I panicked.

How would I tell him the truth and make him understand that everything I did, I did for my family? I prayed that he cared enough about me to accept the truth.

I raised my other hand to smooth out the wrinkles in his baby blue shirt. He wore no undershirt beneath it, so my fingers explored unhindered. Moving my hand up along his arm, I wrapped my fingers around his large bicep and squeezed. Butterflies took flight in my abdomen and soared when he smoothed out my hair. Raising my head to meet his stare, I watched as tiny sparks of yellow danced in his dark green eyes.

I made his eyes heat up like that. Me. Not Ava Grady, me—the woman in front of him. I felt power surge inside of me and I wanted to test my ability to assert it with someone I trusted. I wanted to do something I always wanted to do but was too afraid of being judged for it. Keeping my eyes on his, I ran my hand down his pants and flicked open the button. His eyes widened and his lips parted. Rising on my tiptoes, I placed my lips over his and slowly slid my tongue across his bottom lip.

"Sir, I'm walking to the mayor's office right now," a voice on the speaker shouted from the office phone.

Oh, no! I'd forgotten all about Colton's call. So had Colton.

He swore under his breath.

"Do you want to stay on the line, sir? I'll be there in less than two minutes?" asked the man. I didn't realize how much the thought of someone hearing us excited me. I never thought of myself as a sexual person before, but I felt myself awakening to the possibilities.

I cupped Colton through his pants. "Yes," he hissed.

"Okay, great. Just hold on a minute," said the clerk.

"No problem," I mouthed and squeezed.

Colton smiled and let out a strangled laugh.

"Did you say something, sir?"

"No. Just tell me when you're standing in front of the mayor."

There was a window behind us, but my desk was the only one in front of Colton's office. Still, I didn't want to take a chance. I walked up to the blinds and shut them. Then I added a sway to my hips as I walked back and dropped to my knees.

Unzipping his pants, I released him into the palm of my hand. I'd never imagined doing this with anyone, never wanted to, until now. I licked my lips and ran my tongue along the length of him. He threw his head back but made no sound until I took him into my mouth. I knew I should stop, but I was too aroused to care.

Colton took my hand, raised me up, and led me to his desk. He kissed my lips and reached for the hem of my shirt, but I stopped him. I had every intention of fulfilling my newest fantasy. With both palms to his chest, I pushed him down onto his office chair. A thrill ran through my body as I took hold of him again. Colton hissed when I circled my lips around him and either the clerk hadn't heard him or he thought it best not to mention it. I licked until my own body throbbed and I hummed in pleasure.

Colton ran his fingers down my hair and gently pushed his hips up, asking me to take him deeper. Relaxing my jaw, I pulled him in further. He swore so violently that my cheeks heated.

"Stop," he whispered. I peeked up at him. A tiny bead of sweat danced on his brow. "I'm going to come."

I thought that was the point, so I persisted. His chest heaved until his breaths were rough. He was definitely close.

"Fuuuuck," Colton swore again, louder this time, and his warm seed spilled into my mouth.

"I'm almost there, sir. I'm so sorry to keep you waiting," said the clerk.

With both hands covering his face, Colton shook his head. I rose to my feet, watching a smile twitch on Colton's lips.

"I'm here, sir. I'm just about to go inside his office." Muffled voices intoned in the background until a man's voice boomed over the speaker. "Crawford, is that you?"

Resting his arms behind his head, staring at me with a look I couldn't read, Colton responded. "Yeah, it's me."

"Look, I know you're upset about the delay, but I've got a number of things to take care of. Just this one time, I'll go ahead and sign these now." The sound of a pen scratching paper echoed in the background. "There. Are you happy now?"

"Gordon, you've no fucking clue how happy I am right now."

I covered my laugh with my hand and walked over to Colton's fully stocked washroom. By the time I returned to his office, he stood with his arms crossed, staring out his window.

"Is everything all right?" I asked.

He nodded but kept his gaze outside. I worried perhaps we had passed a boundary by having sex at work. I didn't regret it, though. It was the craziest thing I'd ever done, and the little voice that usually told me to be wary, instead, jumped with her fist up in the air.

I stood in front of him, trying to read his face. When he finally looked at me, he said, "I want you to meet my brothers."

Surprised by his statement, I didn't know how to respond. "But I've already met Ryan."

"Not as an employee of Crawford Corp, but as..."

Don't say it.

I would crumble if he did.

"As your friend?" I suggested.

He smiled and shook his head. "We both know you're much more than that. I know it's been less than two weeks, but this feels right, Ava," he said. And the name pierced right through my heart.

"I don't think that's a good idea," I whispered.

"Why not?"

"Because it's still early and I don't want anyone to know about us, especially because I really need this job."

He laughed. "No one's going to fire you. You may get a raise, though."

"No, no raises," I chuckled because, besides the fact that I wouldn't even be here to receive them, my conscience couldn't take any more.

"Let's take it slow, Colton," I said, interlacing my fingers with his.

"This is the first time I've heard that line not coming from my mouth," he said. "But I can do that for you."

He raised my hand to his lips and kissed my fingers. "How about you come to my place for dinner? I'll invite my brothers and just say you're someone special. It won't be a lie."

This whole arrangement is a lie!

But that wasn't true either. What I felt for Colton wasn't fake. I'd never been more open with a man in my life. This felt like the real Frances Netto. Not that invisible person I'd been for the last five years. *Do it!* The tiny voice in my head shouted.

"No one else, right? Just your two brothers?"

"I promise, just the people that are closest to me in this world, and that includes you."

How could I say no to that? When he held my hand and stared into my eyes like I was his world, how could any woman say no to that?

"Yes," I said.

A grin spread across his face and I think a tiny voice in his head must have whooped because he inhaled deeply right before his lips pressed against mine.

"I'll pick you up tomorrow night at seven," he said, pulling away.

"Um, I have a ton of work to do. Why don't you just pick me up from the office?"

"I don't want you working late."

"It's all right. I prefer to get it done."

"Fine," he said and kissed me again. "I'll see you tomorrow."

I turned to walk out of his office when his voice stopped me. "Oh, Ava?"

I closed my eyes but didn't turn around. "Yes?"

"Tell your family you'll be late. I plan to thank you for your surprise this afternoon. I feel very appreciative right now."

A shiver ran through my body and my legs wobbled as I walked back to my desk.

10

Colton

I performed the same ritual each time I entered my office. I turned on my laptop, checked my stock numbers, and scanned four local auction websites for any new items. Two pieces were still missing from my mother's jewelry collection and I wouldn't stop until I found them. I hired a private investigator to look into this as well, but it steadied my nerves to check the sites each morning. It had taken me nearly twenty years to recover fifteen pieces from the collection and cost me close to a million dollars.

I've been searching for the last two pieces for more than a year, so I nearly fell off my chair when the eighteen-karat gold alligator bracelet appeared in an upcoming auction search. It had six brilliant-cut diamonds totaling three carats, and the estimated sale price was twenty-five thousand dollars. I zoomed in on the inside of the bracelet. Just like every piece before it, the initials JC were engraved: Jaclynn Crawford—my mother's name. This was certainly her bracelet and nearly the last piece from her stolen collection.

I dialed the PI's number. He answered my call after just one ring. "Crawford? How can I help you?"

"I think I found another one," I said. "I need you to go down to

Harrington's and secure this piece. I'm sending you a picture of it now." I emailed him a photo of the bracelet.

"Got it," he said. "I'll take care of it for you."

As soon as I hung up the phone, another call rang through. This one was internal and I smiled.

"How can I help you, Ms. Grady?" I said, leaning back in my chair.

"Colton, I need three hundred dollars," she said, her voice steady.

Swiveling my chair to face the window, I watched her staring at her computer, her finger scrolling on the mouse. She wore a tan dress today and it drove me crazy. I usually preferred to pick out gifts for women, but I liked that Ava was being more forthright.

"All right," I said. Then, visualizing some red lingerie, I added, "Is this something I can rip off of you?"

"No! Gawd, no. It's for a baby's christening."

I didn't think I could lose an erection that quickly.

"What?" I dropped my forearm onto my desk. "What baby?"

She blew out a frustrated breath, as though I were the one talking in riddles. "Robert Morgan's daughter had a baby recently and this weekend is the christening. I thought it would be a good gesture for you to send a gift."

"Oh." I was about to dismiss the idea when I saw its merit. Morgan was a family man and he appreciated the gift Ava gave his dog. I wondered how grateful he'd be if I sent a gift to his granddaughter.

"Yes. Go ahead."

"Thanks."

"How did you know?" I asked, then it hit me. "Social media?"

"Yep," she said. "I follow his daughter and she posted something this morning. I don't think anyone else will know about it but you."

"Good work, Ms. Grady."

"Thank you, Mr. Crawford."

"Now, why don't you come in here so I can thank you properly?"

"Sir, that may take longer than you have time for," she said and hung up the phone. Still staring at her through my office window, she turned to face me and covered her mouth to hide a grin, but she couldn't hide her eyes from smiling, though. Despite the distance, they danced with joy. I wanted to make her smile like that every day for the rest of my life.

Ugh! There I go again, thinking of the future. This woman had me saying and doing things I'd never thought I would.

I remained in my office for the rest of the day. Now that I had the mayor's approval of our plans, it was time to push Morgan with our project. Everything lined up and I could already see the Crawford Corp sign staked on Morgan's property. I imagined excavators digging up the land for the largest shopping mall this town had ever seen. Ava would stand next to me when we cut the ribbon. She would definitely look better cutting the damn thing than I would. Yes, Ava wearing that same tan dress would do the honors.

"Knock, knock." Ryan tapped on my door. "What's got you smiling?" he asked, taking a seat in front of my desk.

"Just picturing our sign on Morgan's property," I said.

"Are you sure it has nothing to do with the pretty brunette across the hallway?"

I smirked. "It might," I admitted, then stood from my desk. Opening the top drawer, I pulled out a set of keys and threw them at Ryan. "Here."

He caught them and stared at the logo. With a frown, he asked, "You went on a date?"

"Yep," I said and sat back down. I didn't even care that I'd given up my car or lost another stupid bet with Ryan. Huh, funny that. I smiled thinking of Ava's reaction when I took her with me to find a new car.

"Man, I've never seen you like this." Ryan crossed his arms and stared at me.

"Like what?"

"Smiling and shit."

I scowled. "I smile, Ryan."

"No, you don't. Like never. Not even when you find one of mom's lost pieces of jewelry do you smile."

"They weren't lost. They were stolen."

He put his hands up. "Forget I brought it up." Then, crossing his arms, he asked, "Did you sleep with her?"

"That's none of your business," I said.

"So that's a yes." Dropping into the armchair, he added, "Sleeping with an employee, Colton? This could be trouble."

"No, it's not. So don't make any."

He sighed, then jerked his head up. "Have you invited her to join us for dinner tonight?"

"I did." Then I leaned forward toward him, my finger pointed at him. "And you make her feel welcomed."

He gave a small smile. "I'm looking forward to getting acquainted with the woman who's made you happy for the first time in your miserable life."

I couldn't even argue with Ryan. I had been a miserable bastard.

"You'll like her. She's genuine and smart," I said.

"I already like her," he said. Then, pursing his lips, he asked. "Have you done a background check on her yet?"

My brothers and I often attracted the wrong kind of people, those looking to trap us into marriage or steal information from us for some business adversary.

"Nah. She's not like that. Like I said, she's the real deal."

Ryan nodded. "Just in case, do you mind if I do?"

For some strange reason, I didn't like Ryan checking up on Ava as though she was some gold-digging con artist. But if I fought him on this, I had no leg to stand on if I ever had suspicions about someone he dated. Knowing he'd find nothing anyway, I conceded.

"Go right ahead. Waste your time and money," I said.

He stood and buttoned his suit jacket. "I'll see you later tonight."

I waved him off and resumed my work.

Frances

The empty office was eerily quiet except for the heating fan that would come on every twenty minutes. I wrapped up the last of my files and walked over to the bathroom to freshen up. After reapplying my lipstick, I checked my phone. It was a quarter to seven, and Colton said he'd send a car for me at this time. Snapping the cap back on the tube, I gave my hair one last shake and headed out.

A black sedan waited for me outside the office building. The driver stepped out when he saw me. "Good evening, Ms. Grady?"

"Good evening, Eric." I was getting used to identifying with the name. It wasn't a good thing.

Watching the apartment buildings recede and large estate-like homes take their place, I wondered which street Eric had turned on. I'd never seen homes like this in the city before. Large trees and rocks accented the properties, and lights illuminated all four corners of the home—considering the size of these homes, it was more like twelve corners.

"Where are we?" I asked.

"We're in Forest Hill," he said.

I'd heard of the neighborhood, but I'd never actually been here. I guessed there weren't many bus routes along these streets.

Eric pulled into a cement driveway that led to a modern-inspired home. A glass balcony protruded from the side, on top of three garages. Two large black doors with long steel handles dwarfed me at the entrance, the top of the handle reaching my eyebrows. *Who lived here? Giants?*

The overbearing doors opened before I could even knock. Colton stood in the middle of what I could only describe as a museum with white columns and glass accents all around.

"Hey," he said and kissed my cheek when I ventured to step inside.

"Hi."

Staring at the tall windows all around me, I asked, "How did you know I was here? I didn't even ring the doorbell."

"I received a notification on my phone that someone was at my front door."

Of course he did.

The only notifications I ever received were angry shouts from my grandmother to answer the door.

"Please come in," he said.

I wanted to take off my shoes like I always did at home. But Colton wore his shoes instead of socks, so I left mine on. My heels tapped on the white porcelain floor and the sound echoed throughout the house. I bet there were ten bedrooms upstairs. I shuddered thinking of cleaning this place, then chuckled, realizing those who lived in such a home rarely cleaned it themselves.

"Do you like it?" asked a voice to my left. Not realizing I was still looking up at the second floor, I turned to face Colton's brother, Ryan.

"Oh, hi! Yes, I do. Very much so," I said and smiled.

"It's quite impressive," he said and watched me as my eyes hungrily took in every piece of artwork.

"Wow, is that a Cecily Brown piece?" I asked.

"It is," said Colton. "I didn't know you were a connoisseur of art."

"Well, you've only known her, what, ten days?" asked Ryan. "I'm sure there's a lot you still don't know about her."

Colton shot Ryan a glare, but I wasn't offended. I hadn't mentioned my love of art to him before. "I love modern pieces, and this is one of my favorites."

"Mine too," said Colton, and tiny creases appeared beside his eyes when he smiled.

"Can I get you something to drink, Ava?" asked Ryan.

"Whatever you have is fine," I said, wanting to deflect any further attention from me. The employees at Crawford Corp thought Ryan was the nicer of the two brothers, but I didn't like the way he watched me earlier. Like I was some puzzle he was trying to figure out.

Colton guided me along the hallway, and when we turned the corner, a young man, wearing a white t-shirt and jeans, stood over the stove, sprinkling salt over a pan.

"This is my youngest brother, Luke," said Colton.

Luke wiped his hands on a towel and shook my hand. "Pleasure to meet you, Ava," he said.

"Luke is the chef of the family. Insisted on cooking the meal himself tonight. I usually order out for us," explained Colton.

"I hope you didn't go to too much trouble on my account," I said, feeling a lot more nervous than I was earlier.

"Not at all. I do it out of pity for these two fools that don't eat a home-cooked meal unless I make it." A dimple appeared on his left cheek when he winked at me.

I liked him.

"Save your charm for someone else," said Colton, steering me away from his brother. "He knows how much people love that he cooks better than a chef at a Michelin star restaurant."

"Dinner will be served in just a few minutes," said Luke, turning off the stove and pulling open the oven door.

"Here, let me help you," I said, pivoting out of Colton's arm and reaching for the oven mitt in Luke's hand. Setting the table and serving were my specialty since *Nonna* and Marco did most of the cooking. I put on the mitt and grabbed the silver-domed pot inside. Placing the pot on top of the stove, I lifted the lid. Hot steam rose from the inside and the aroma of reduced wine, rosemary and garlic warmed my palette and tempted my appetite. "That smells incredible," I said, closing my eyes and inhaling deeper.

"Knew we should have ordered in," mumbled Colton.

"Is this a top sirloin roast?" I asked, looking at the perfectly browned meat inside.

"You know your cuts," said Luke. He passed me a white serving dish and tongs while he stirred a pot. I carefully placed the sirloin on the dish and added a few scoops of jus to the dish. Luke poured a pan of roasted potatoes onto another plate and passed a bowl of salad to Ryan. "Here, put this on the table."

"Follow me," said Luke as he led me through a smaller kitchen and into the dining room. A silver chandelier hung over a white marble table. A white and yellow flower arrangement sat in the center of the table and I gently placed the sirloin next to it.

"Let's eat," grinned Luke.

Colton pulled out a chair and sat next to me, while Ryan and Luke took seats across from us.

"Thank you for inviting me. This all looks so wonderful," I said.

"The pleasure is ours," said Colton, and squeezed my hand. I blushed, embarrassed by Colton's display of affection when we were supposed to be just friends in front of his brothers.

"Let go of her hand and let the woman eat," said Luke, making my blush deepen.

One bite of the roast and my mouth hummed with pleasure. The seasoning wasn't overdone. There was just enough salt and black pepper to bring out the flavor of the sirloin. "This is exquisite," I said.

"Not bad," said Luke, taking another bite.

"So, Ava, tell me," began Ryan. "How long have you worked as a personal assistant?" The morsel of sirloin sank to the pit of my stomach.

"Um, ten days," I said, trying to be as honest as possible.

Luke and Colton laughed, but Ryan didn't.

"You must have had an impressive education or other for Colton to hire you." Then, turning to his brother, he asked, "What was it about her resume you found intriguing?"

Colton poured me a glass of wine and then did the same for himself. "I don't recall," he said. "But looks like it all worked out quite well, didn't it?"

Ryan stared at me, and I wondered, did he know something? Did he pull Ava Grady's resume out of the trash? If so, why wait until now to bring it up? No, he was probably just making conversation. I was being paranoid.

"What do you do in your spare time? Any extra-curricular activities? Church groups?" asked Ryan, leaning across the table.

Church groups? Ava's resume mentioned something about that, didn't it? But I couldn't be sure.

I cleared my throat and thought fast. "God's work is something I do privately. Besides, humility is a virtue, is it not?"

"Indeed, it is," said Ryan. "Are you a virtuous woman, Ava?"

"Ryan!" Colton slammed his fork onto the table.

"Ignore my brother," said Luke, shooting Ryan a glare. "Even when he's not working, he likes to put everyone on the stand."

I laughed nervously and resumed eating. Slowly, I cut a tiny bite of the steak, hoping it would slide down my constricted throat. It didn't work. I swallowed with difficulty and washed it down with a gulp of wine. Ryan suspected something. I needed to end this tonight. Before anyone found out the truth.

Turning to Colton, I said, "I'm feeling a little unwell. Do you mind taking me home?"

Colton raised his eyes and fired a stare at his brother. Ryan flinched, if only a little.

"You don't have to leave, Ava," said Ryan. "I apologize if I made you uncomfortable."

Patting my mouth with the white napkin, I waited for my heart to stop hammering in my chest before I stood from the table. "Apology accepted. But I'm afraid I do need to get going." If I stayed any longer, the nerves in my stomach would toss up my dinner.

"I'll drive Ava home and be right back," said Colton, then pointed a finger at Ryan. "Don't leave until I get back. I need a word with you." Ryan nodded.

"It was very nice to meet you," I said, turning to Luke. "The meal was delicious."

"Too bad you couldn't stay for dessert," he said and softened the reminder with a smile.

I was going to say some other time, but the words wouldn't push through my lips. Would there be another time? I would quit in less than two days and then I'd be back to my invisible self.

"What's your address?" asked Colton when we climbed into his car. I hesitated for a moment, wondering if I would give myself away by telling him my address, but realized if he didn't remember what was on Ava's resume, I doubted he recalled where she lived. So, I gave it to him and we set off.

Sitting in Colton's car, away from Ryan's perceptive stare, my shoulders relaxed and my adrenaline subsided. I finally took a deep breath without it feeling like my ribs would break. Colton hadn't said a word since we left his place, and neither did I until I pointed to my house. "It's that one over there, with the red bricks," I said.

He pulled into the driveway and turned off the engine. I turned to face him, wanting to apologize for ending the night abruptly.

"I'm so sorry about tonight," he said, surprising me.

"Don't apologize," I told him. "It wasn't your fault."

It's mine for lying in the first place.

"Ryan has no excuse but perhaps I could offer an explanation," he began, but I raised my hand to cut him off.

"You don't have to explain," I said, guilt replacing fear. Colton didn't need to explain anything to me.

But he persisted. "Please, I want you to know that it's nothing personal toward you. When we lost our parents, we took it upon ourselves to protect each other. I made sure our physical needs were met, a roof over our heads, and food on the table. Ryan would talk us out of any trouble we got ourselves into and Luke, well, Luke could charm almost anyone to do his bidding. Don't get me wrong, I'm mad as hell at Ryan right now and I'll tell him so, but I understand why he did it."

"I get it. I really do," I explained. Then, closing my eyes, I admitted something to Colton I had never even acknowledged to myself. "I don't like confrontation. It terrifies me, actually. I prefer people don't see me at all rather than have to defend myself." My hands trembled as I spoke, but I clasped them between my thighs. It was difficult to express in words one of my greatest fears aloud. I hadn't expected to say it, and I didn't feel any better acknowledging it right now. I felt embarrassed.

My chest tightened and I worried I would have a panic attack in the car in front of Colton. He must have realized something was going on with me because the next moment Colton unbuckled my seat belt and pulled me into his arms. I clutched his shoulder and valiantly held back tears, but not a quick intake of air. The breath pierced my stiff lungs and I trembled in his embrace.

"Hey," he crooned, rubbing my back. "You shouldn't have to defend yourself, especially not to my family."

He held me tighter, then added, "And you handled yourself pretty great back there with my brother. Confrontation isn't about arguing or yelling, it's about holding your own. Sometimes walking away is the best way to defend yourself from a bad situation."

He had no idea how much his words meant to me. Walking away tonight was one of the hardest things I'd done in six years. Back then, I'd left to preserve myself. Tonight's motivation was less honorable. I owed Colton so much, but most of all, I owed him the truth.

"Colton—"

He pressed his lips against mine, stopping my words. Gently, he kissed my mouth, coaxing his tongue inside. I mewled from the pleasure of it.

"I love you," he whispered.

The words broke my heart and shattered it into tiny pieces. I loved him too, but before I could say those words, I had to tell him so much more. All of it, and prayed that he would understand. If he had truly fallen in love with me, he would understand, wouldn't he?

"Colton—" I said again. His lips moved to my jaw and he inhaled. I closed my eyes and hoped I wasn't about to make a mistake.

Then I saw him. Marco stood in front of the car with his arms crossed over his chest. It was freezing outside, and yet he wore only a sweater with his sleeves pushed up. Standing under six feet tall, Marco's large arms were more intimidating than his height. I'd never seen my brother look so menacing. I'd be impressed if I wasn't about to perish from fear. This isn't how I wanted Colton to find out the truth about me. Not from Marco's lips. I imagined jumping out of the car and dragging Marco to the front door to get him away from here.

"I've got to go," I said, opening the car door. But Colton stepped out as well.

"I'll walk you to your door," he said.

Why did he have to be chivalrous at this moment?

"No, it's fine," I said, getting out of the car and running straight for Marco. "I'll see you at work tomorrow." *Dammit, why did I say that?*

Still staring at Colton, Marco asked, "Is this guy your boss?"

I tried to push Marco toward the front door, but he didn't budge.

"Her boyfriend," said Colton.

Can a heart soar and break at the same time? Mine did.

Colton raised his hand toward my brother. "My name's Colton Crawford. And you are?"

I turned a weak smile toward Colton. "This is my brother."

"Marco," he responded and shook Colton's hand.

I watched as the two men sized each other up, Marco blatantly looking over at Colton's expensive car and then his shoes, while Colton stared at the tendons shooting from Marco's hand to his forearm.

"It's a pleasure to meet you," said Colton. Despite the age difference—Colton was more than ten years older than Marco—he didn't talk down to him.

"Yes, well, thank you for the ride, but I better get going." This time, when I nudged Marco, he allowed me to lead him to the door. Although, I still had to drag him by the wrist.

"See you tomorrow, Ava," said Colton, and climbed back into his car.

"*Ava*?" Marco asked, staring at me. "Why did he call you Ava? What are you playing at, Frannie?"

My heart stopped, but now was not the time to explain everything to Marco. Colton deserved the truth first. "Nothing. It's all a misunderstanding that I plan to clear up tomorrow. I promise. Now can we go inside? It's been a long night."

11

Frances

The night had grown longer still as I tossed and turned, trying to think of the right words to explain the situation to Colton. I thought the hardest part would be keeping my own feelings in check. I'd never imagined Colton falling for someone like me. Invisible Frannie.

As I dressed and came downstairs, I rehearsed what I would say. "Colton, I only meant to help my brother... I was only supposed to be your assistant... I hadn't planned to fall in love."

Marco and *Nonna* were making breakfast in the kitchen as usual, but it surprised me to find my mother at the table peeling potatoes.

"Mom, what are you doing at home?" I rarely saw either of my parents. They both worked at least two jobs. Sometimes we'd all watch a movie together on the weekend. But we hadn't done that in quite some time.

"They cut my shift at the restaurant in half. The owner's granddaughter needs a job to pay for her first car. Says he wants to teach her the value of making money. It's a good lesson. So, she will take my shifts."

My mom pursed her lips, as though she held back some emotion, but she never showed it. She was too proud, even to call her boss unfair. "I'll just check with Mrs. Nguyen and see if she needs a new cleaner for her office," she continued.

"A third job, mom. Really?" I asked.

"Yes, Francesca. We do what we have to. I'll have plenty of time to rest when I'm dead." She had said this to me before. Only this time, her smile didn't reach her eyes.

"I have to go," I said, grabbing a banana and heading out the door.

"Do you want me to drive you?" asked Marco.

"No. The bus is fine."

I couldn't take another moment in front of my mother, knowing I was about to walk away from a job that paid me both of our salaries combined. But it really wasn't mine to keep. I hoped I'd done enough at work that Colton would consider keeping me on, and perhaps his feelings for me would help, too.

When I reached the office, Erika was on the phone, so I simply waved to her and headed to my desk. Colton had his office door closed, but I saw him pacing back and forth, talking to someone on the phone.

I wanted to get this conversation with Colton over with before I lost the nerve. Turning on my computer, I checked my email, hoping to distract myself while Colton was busy. But no matter how many times I read the first line of an email, my mind wandered to the words I would say to explain everything.

Colton, I didn't mean for this to happen. No, that wasn't exactly true.

Colton, funny story... No, he wouldn't appreciate the humor in this situation.

Colton, I'm so sorry...

A movement caught my attention. Colton hung up the phone and turned toward his laptop. Rising from my desk, I smoothed out my beige skirt and knocked on his door. *Lead with the heart, Frances!*

"Come in," he said but continued to stare at his screen.

"Colton, can we talk?"

"Of course, but can you hold that thought until lunch? Shit just hit the fan with the Sandig project and I need to clean it up before it gets any worse."

While I wanted to talk now, I knew it'd be better when he wasn't worried about losing a client. "No problem," I said. "I'll see you later."

Closing the door behind me, I considered walking over to Erika to help settle my nerves, but she was chatting with Athena from the mailroom. I spun on my heels before Athena could see me. I didn't think she'd recognize me, but I didn't want to tempt fate so close to me revealing the truth.

Get a grip, Frances. You will speak to him soon, and all the pretenses will be done.

Needing a few minutes to pull myself together, I walked over to the bathroom. My palms were sweaty and perspiration gathered at the nape of my neck. I pulled my hair to the side and splashed some cold water just below my hairline. Droplets of water ran down my back, cooling me further. Inhaling a large breath, I released it slowly.

Everything will be fine.

The bathroom door swung open, and Colton walked in.

"Are you alone?" he asked.

I peeked at the two empty stalls and nodded my head. He reached me in two steps and gathered me into his arms. He kissed me until my head spun. I wrapped my arms around his neck, steadying myself.

"I've been yelling and cursing all morning. I needed a moment to hold someone good and decent. Unlike those bloodsucking lawyers."

"Colton—"

"Shh, I don't want to talk. I just want to kiss you before my next call."

My knees felt weak and my face scrunched up, fighting back tears.

"Colton, we have to talk," I said again.

"We will." He checked his watch. "I promise. Just not right here, not now. I've got to go." He kissed my lips and left as quickly as he'd come. This man destroyed me even when he loved me. And I couldn't even blame him for it.

When I pushed open the bathroom door, I glanced down the hallway to see if anyone was watching. Fortunately, the girl whose cubicle was located nearest to the washroom was not at her desk. But my temporary relief at not being discovered in the washroom with Colton soon turned to fear. Standing by the elevators, holding a brown paper bag, was Marco.

Oh, no, no, no! Of all the days for Marco to visit me at work.

I peeked at Colton's office, but he was already on the phone again and facing the large window. His back to me, I raced down the hallway before he could turn around.

"What are you doing here?" I hissed. Then a thought popped into my mind and I panicked. "How'd you know to find me on the twelfth floor?"

"You forgot your sandwich this morning. When I didn't see you in the mailroom, I came to the twelfth floor to ask Erika if she knew where you were." Marco peeked over my shoulder, grinning at my best friend. While she smiled back, Erika didn't look up but continued typing on her keyboard. Turning back to me, Marco added, "I thought you'd appreciate me dropping it off."

I grabbed the bag. "Thank you," I said. "Now, please leave. This isn't a good time."

"Now is a great time, actually," said Erika. "Go grab a coffee with your brother next door."

I pulled Erika aside. "I can't go now. I need to speak to Colton," I whispered.

"He's going to be in those meetings at least until noon. Take a break and a breath. You won't get any work done this morning, anyway. You've been staring at the same blank email all morning."

"You couldn't possibly see that from down here," I hissed.

Erika crossed her arms. "Prove me wrong."

I couldn't, so I fumed instead. "Fine." Grabbing Marco's arm, I pulled him toward the elevator and jammed my finger against the button. Fortunately, the doors opened and we stepped inside before anyone else noticed us.

"What's gotten into you, Frannie?" Marco asked when the doors closed.

"This job has me a little worked up, that's all."

"Well, dating the boss may have something to do with it."

"Hey!" I scolded him as we exited the elevator and walked through the main foyer. He may have been right about dating the boss, but I was still his older sister. "I've got this. And it isn't what it looks like."

Walking past the mailroom door, I stole a glance through the window. I spotted Clive chatting with a colleague. I imagined myself beside him next week—everything back to the way it was before I'd met Colton. I hated the image.

The café was attached to our building but had a separate entrance. It wasn't very busy at ten-thirty in the morning, but the space was quite large with an open twenty-foot ceiling. There were three customers in line and a few more sat at tables with their drinks and laptops in front of them. The aroma of freshly brewed coffee improved my mood as I walked toward a table in the back.

"What's going on, Fran?" asked Marco as soon as we sat down.

I inhaled deeply and debated whether or not to tell Marco the truth. Today was the day I would come clean, so might as well start now. "I lied."

"About what?"

I sighed. "Everything."

"You have to be a little more specific than that."

I sat up straight in my chair and emptied my conscience. "I lied to you when I said I got an advance instead of a new job. I lied to Colton to get the new PA job. I lied to myself when I said this would be easy and I can pull it off."

Drained from the relief of finally saying it all out loud, I dropped my head into my arms on top of the table.

"What do you mean you lied to Colton to get the job? Did you fudge your resume?"

"No, that's just it. It wasn't even my resume. I stood in his office holding some other woman's resume, and he assumed it was me. He hired me on the spot." I wasn't sure if Marco heard my muffled explanation while my head was still in my arms.

"Well… you didn't really lie to him then."

I sat up and crossed my arms. Tilting my head to the side, I asked with my voice laced with skepticism, "Really? You wouldn't consider that lying?"

His lips twitched, but he kept them in check. "Um… well, more like a misunderstanding."

I smiled this time. I loved my brother for trying to defend me. "Only, I hadn't corrected him. I took the job instead, knowing I would quit in two weeks. I lied."

"Why two weeks?"

"That's when I would have enough money to pay for your first semester at college."

All humor drained from his face. "You did this for me?"

I nodded, then slapped a hand to my forehead and groaned, "Now I have to go up there and tell Colton the truth."

"Why?" His question sounded genuine.

Narrowing my eyes, I asked, "What do you mean why?"

"Why tell him now, when you only have two more days until you finish what you've started?"

"You don't understand. This has turned into something more than just a job. He's not some jerk I'm pulling a fast one over. I care for him and..."

"And?" asked Marco, reaching for my hand.

"And he told me he loved me." My voice cracked on the last word. I pressed my lips together, holding them firmly with my teeth.

Marco grabbed my hand across the table. "If he loves you, Frannie, he'll understand."

Nodding, I agreed. "That's what I'm hoping. That we can move past this. That when I explain everything to him, he'll know why I did it and forgive me."

He gave my hand one last squeeze before he leaned back in his chair. "I know he will. You're a good person, Frannie."

A small weight had been lifted from my chest simply from unburdening myself with Marco. I couldn't wait to speak to Colton and finally put this all behind us.

I hugged Marco and said goodbye. Walking out of the coffee shop, I squared my shoulders and marched back to the office, ready for what I had to do. Marco was right, Colton would understand. Look how quickly Marco grasped that it was all just a simple misunderstanding. I'd been making myself sick with worry when I just had to trust that things were going to work out for me this time. I had someone who believed in me and wanted what was best for me.

Stepping off the elevator on the twelfth floor, I noticed Erika was on the phone, so I walked directly to my cubicle, but heard her call my name. I turned around. Putting a hand over the phone's receiver, she said, "Wait up. We need to talk."

I waved her off, determined that nothing was going to stop me now. "Yes. I just need to have one other conversation first."

"Fran," she whispered, but I ignored her and marched down the hallway. Setting down my purse, I turned to Colton's office. Two people sat in front of his desk, but I couldn't make out who they were since the blinds hid them quite well.

My phone rang. It was Colton.

"Yes, Mr. Crawford," I said with a smile.

"I need to see you in my office," he bit out and hung up the phone.

His tone made the hair on the back of my neck rise, but I shook it off. He'd been in one meeting after another this morning and a new problem probably just fell onto his lap. Grabbing my notepad and pencil, I walked into his office, ready to work. Our conversation could wait until later. He needed me right now.

"What can I do for you?" I asked, staring at Colton.

Waving his hand toward the person sitting in the chair in front of him, he said, "I'd like you to meet someone."

I turned to face the visitor. The woman stood, her black dress and blazer falling mid-thigh. She raised her hand toward me, but both of mine were full.

With a smile, she announced, "I'm Ava Grady."

12

Colton

When her face fell and her eyes rounded, I knew it was true. I didn't want to believe Ryan and this woman, but I couldn't deny Ava's reaction.

She's not Ava. That's not her name.

I didn't even know her real name. We were intimate together and she didn't even tell me her real name. Anger ignited inside me, deep in the pit of my stomach, where it had simmered since I was a young boy. I had promised myself I wouldn't let anyone fool me again.

She dropped her pencil and crouched down to retrieve it. "I can explain," she said as she rose to her feet and turned to me. She had addressed me, but I couldn't look at her. I didn't trust what would come out of my mouth. I wanted to shout at her, then beg her to tell me the truth. But how could I believe a word that came from her mouth? I stared at Ryan instead. He raised his eyebrows and tilted his head, waiting for me to make the next move.

"I don't want to hear it," I said.

"Colton," she whispered my name like a plea.

Finally turning toward her, I asked, "Is your name Ava Grady or not?"

She shook her head, her brown curls framing her stricken face. "No, it's Frances Netto."

That was all I needed to hear. I had been conned again, only this time they hadn't taken any jewels. She had stolen something I'd never thought I would lose—my heart. Shame, combined with my anger, formed a volcano inside me that finally erupted.

"Get out," I shouted. She flinched, nodded once, then turned to leave.

"Wait," Ryan called out. "How did you get past security in the building?"

"I work in the mailroom downstairs," she said. Turning those pleading brown eyes toward Ryan, she continued, "I didn't mean—"

"Worked," I said, controlling my rage with deep breaths.

"Pardon?" She turned slowly to face me.

"You *worked* in the mailroom downstairs. I don't ever want you stepping foot inside Crawford Corp again. Now. Get. Out." I knew if she stayed another minute, I would bend and listen to her pleas. But I wouldn't be made a fool again.

Her lips quivered, but she pressed down on them. She nodded again and left my office. I watched her grab her purse and walk toward the reception desk. Ryan's words interrupted my gaze.

"Looks like the position is available again. Should you still wish to work for Crawford Corp, Ms. Grady. I hope this incident hasn't changed your mind."

She smiled. It was a perfect smile. Straight, over whitened teeth, against sunbed-kissed skin. She didn't have a slight overbite that made her lips pout naturally, like Av—. I had to stop thinking of her as Ava. I had to stop thinking of her. Period.

"Yes, thank you. I can begin in two weeks."

"Tomorrow," I said absently, still staring down the hallway. I couldn't see the reception desk from here, but I was sure she must have stepped into the elevators by now.

"I'm afraid that won't be possible," said the woman. I couldn't quite think of her as Ava yet.

"Then I'm afraid I'll have to keep looking. I need someone today, but I'll make tomorrow work." I turned my full attention to her. Best she knew what she was getting herself into now. "Either you start tomorrow or I'll have to find myself a new PA."

"Good luck with that, Mr. Crawford. You're gonna need it." She buttoned her blazer and turned to leave.

"Wait." Ryan glared at me and shook his head. "We'll hire a PA from the temp agency to cover the next two weeks. We can appreciate that you need to give your current employer notice."

"Thank you, Mr. Crawford. I look forward to working with you," she said. Then to me, she narrowed her eyes and sucked her top teeth before leaving my office.

"That went well," said Ryan, dropping into the armchair, crossing his legs in a relaxed posture. My muscles tensed from restraining myself from running after her. She may only be in the foyer by now. No. I would not chase after someone who lied to me. Tricked me.

I unfurled my fists, not realizing I had curled them in the first place, and sat at my desk.

"How did you figure it out?" I asked, wanting it over with. Better to pull the figurative knife out of my heart at once so the wound could heal.

"After our dinner, I did a little digging. It wasn't difficult. A quick internet search pulled up a couple of social media posts from two people named Ava Grady. Neither of them looked like Frances."

Knowing that it was her name didn't make it any easier to hear.

"So, I messaged them both and asked if they had recently applied for the PA position at Crawford Corp. The real Ava Grady messaged me late last night and I asked her to come in this morning."

I nodded.

"You know, you didn't have to fire Frances. She could have continued working in the mailroom. I doubt you would have run into her."

"No. If I know she's downstairs, I don't trust myself not to grab her and..."

"And?"

And kiss her? No. Shake her? No. I didn't know what I'd do. It was best I didn't have to find out.

"And nothing because we will never mention the name Frances Netto again. Do you understand?"

"Perfectly," said Ryan.

"Good. Now get out of my office."

I needed to be alone, if I was lucky, for the rest of my life.

Frances

The coppery taste of blood filled my mouth, but it still didn't stop me from biting my lip, afraid that if I did, a loud sob would follow. I hurried past Erika and frantically pressed the elevator button.

"Frannie! Wait!" she said, coming around the desk.

I shook my head, but when she reached me and put her hands around me, I lost the battle. Tears flowed, and the sob I had so earnestly held back broke free from my mouth.

"Shh, don't let them see you cry." She rubbed my back and then pulled me away.

Her brown eyes held mine and she whispered in a voice that steeled my nerves, "Don't ever let them see you cry."

I nodded. She was right. I wiped away my tears. When the elevator doors opened, I walked in and didn't look back.

On the bus ride home, I watched the office buildings flicker to neighborhoods like flipping the pages of a magazine. Finally, the pawnshop at the corner of my street came into view and I recognized my stop. I took my time walking home; I didn't know what I'd tell my family. Not only didn't I have the money for Marco's first semester, but I also didn't have a job anymore. My family depended on my salary to pay for groceries each week.

As much as that worried me, what pained me the most was having lost Colton. He hated me. And frankly, the way he treated me, I hated him right back. I knew what I'd done was far from professional, but I thought we had something more personal, something real. The way he ordered me to leave, like I was nothing to him, stung. Maybe if I'd told him before he'd found out from his brother, he may have heard me out.

Regardless, it's over and our paths would never cross again.

As I walked through the front door, the scent of garlic and tomatoes drifted into the foyer. It was like serotonin to my brain. It calmed my nerves and comforted me as did my *Nonna's* voice.

"Francesca, is that you?" she asked when I entered the kitchen.

"It's me, *Nonna*."

"You're back early. Everything all right?"

I pushed my lips together again and nodded. "Yep. Everything will be just fine." It had to be. "I have to make a phone call. I'll be down in a few minutes."

An idea popped into my head. Racing up the stairs and into my bedroom, I found the phone number I had jotted down only a couple of weeks ago and dialed the number.

"Hello, Marcus?"

"Yes?"

"It's Frances. I applied for the manager position at your store a couple of weeks ago. Is the job still available?"

"Oh, hi. Yes, I remember you. When you didn't return my calls, I hired someone else. I didn't think you were interested." He was right. I never called him back when I returned from Miami.

"I understand," I said, and swallowed. *Now what?*

I was just about to thank him for his time when he added, "I do have a sales position available. It's yours if you want it."

Oh, no. I couldn't do sales, could I?

I would be front and center with new people all day long and have to put myself out there to get the commission. I didn't think I could do that. But what other choice did I have?

"Yes, I'll take it. Thank you."

It wouldn't be enough to pay for Marco's school, but at least we'd eat.

13

Frances

The store manager, the one who got the job instead of me, shot me a pointed stare as I folded a sweater in the New Arrivals section. She gave me the same look when she caught me organizing the stock in the back room and when I color-coded the jewelry display.

"While I appreciate your work ethic, Frances, your job title is sales associate. You haven't made one sale yet today, have you?" I recalled the elderly lady who wanted to buy a gift for her granddaughter. I suggested a charcoal pencil set after she mentioned how much her granddaughter enjoyed drawing. Unfortunately, our store didn't sell those, so I couldn't make that argument to my manager.

"Not yet. But I'm working on it," I said and managed a weak smile for her.

"Well, you may need to try a new tactic other than organizing. Why don't you go over there and ask that woman if she needs any help?"

I turned in the direction my manager pointed. A tall, blonde woman, around my age, held several pieces of clothing in her arm while she flipped through the dress rack with the other.

"Sure thing," I said and approached the woman. "Hi, there. My name is Frances. Is there anything I can help you with today?"

The pink fingernail that raked through the dresses stopped, and she raised two perfectly shaped eyebrows at me. Her eyes assessed me from head to toe while popping the gum in her mouth.

"Here. You can hold these," she said, handing me the pile of clothes.

"I'll start a change room for you and be right back."

When I returned, she had another armful of clothes ready to try on. "This should do it. Where's my change room?" she asked.

I guided her to the room in the back and helped her with the curtain. "I'll be right out here if you need me."

I smiled at my manager when she gave me the thumbs up. About ten minutes had passed when the woman in the change room called out, "Can you get me a size four in this one? The sizes here are all wrong." She passed me the dress and I went back to the rack. When I couldn't find her size there, I tried the backroom. Finding it, I hurried back to the woman.

"Here you go," I said, and she grabbed the dress through the small opening in the curtain.

"Can you get me a size six in these?" This time she passed me a pair of black leather pants.

"Sure."

When I returned with her pants, she handed me a blouse next. I repeated this for another ten pieces.

Finally, the woman emerged from the change room about an hour later.

"Which items can I take to the register for you?" I asked, looking back to ensure my manager saw the pile of clothing I would bring up to the front.

"None of them," she said. "They were all so drab. Nothing really popped, you understand."

I nodded but had no idea what she was talking about. "Perhaps if you tell me what you need, I can help you find it."

She laughed. "Honey, I don't *need* anything. Something has to call to me. Everything here was too quiet, you know?"

Again, I didn't know, but I nodded anyway.

The woman walked out of the store and I looked at the rack of clothing next to her change room. It would take me another hour just to put everything away. I didn't mind, but I knew my manager wouldn't be pleased.

As expected, she walked right up to me as soon as the customer left. "She didn't buy anything? Not one piece from all those clothes?"

"Not one," I confirmed.

The manager pursed her lips. "What did you say to her?"

Exhausted and confused, I threw my hands in the air and explained, "I didn't say anything."

She pursed her lips. "Maybe that was the problem."

Her words pricked my confidence.

She walked away and I hung a blouse on the rack, my back straight, fighting to keep my head up.

Colton

Ava Grady started work today. Well, the real Ava Grady. The temp was a disaster. She messed up all the filing Frances had organized and never arrived to work on time, not even once over the last ten days. When Ava arrived ten minutes early, I murmured my approval.

"Good morning, Mr. Crawford," she said, stepping into my office. "How was your evening?"

"We can discard the small talk. Let's worry about this afternoon's meeting with Robert Morgan. I need him to sign that deal today."

She puckered her lips and narrowed her eyes as though she'd just bitten into a lemon, but fixed her face quickly.

"Can you get me the Morgan file and email his assistant? Find out what Morgan drinks these days. I want to have a bottle ready for him when he arrives for us to toast." I learned that trick from Frances.

"I don't have an email yet," she said.

"I asked Erika to set one up for you yesterday. I'm sure it's on a note by your desk."

"All right. When will IT be here to set it up for me on my laptop?"

"IT?" I asked, turning to face her. "You just have to plug it into the mail application on your laptop. It'll only take a few minutes."

"That may be true," said Ava. "But that isn't in my job description. My time would be better spent doing what I was hired to do."

I smiled because if I didn't, my voice would probably send her running and I needed her for today's meeting with Morgan. "Ms. Grady, you were hired to assist me. Your job description is to do what I ask of you to do. Now, send that email, and don't let me repeat myself."

This time her lips twitched and her cheeks hollowed as though she were sucking them in. I waited for the usual tears, but she turned on her heel and left instead. Well, not exactly the best start, but at least she didn't walk out.

I spent the next few hours going over the plans, the schedules, the costs, and the profits, ready for anything Morgan would throw at me.

My phone rang at precisely two o'clock. "Yes?" I answered.

"Mr. Morgan is here," said Ava.

"Bring him in."

Hanging up the phone, I rubbed the palm of my hands against my black slacks. I didn't know why I was so nervous. I just knew that I wanted this account more than any other business deal I'd closed so far.

Morgan strode into my office; his belly appeared a little larger than the last time I'd seen him. He reminded me of Colonel Sanders with his white hair and mustache.

"Mr. Morgan, sir," I said, extending my hand. "Pleased to see you again."

Morgan ignored my hand and hooked a thumb behind him. "What happened to your other assistant? The one who brought the cannoli. What was her name again?"

Surprised by his questions, I faltered in my response. I had prepared an answer to any business question he'd throw at me, except for any about Frances.

"Her name's Frances. And, um... she left."

"Really? That's a shame, Crawford. Doesn't bode well for you if you can't keep good staff around."

I pasted on a smile. I didn't want to argue about Frances. "She's on temporary leave," I lied. Wanting to change the subject quickly, I added, "Why don't you take a seat and we can discuss business?"

Morgan sat at the meeting desk in my office. His eyes scanned the room, searching. I connected my laptop to the television monitor in my office and opened the first slide of my presentation.

"Do you have family, Crawford?" Morgan's question surprised me again. The bastard had to know about my brothers. Despite our efforts, we made the news often. I wanted to discuss the business plans I'd put together, not Luke or Ryan.

But I unclenched my fist and said, "Yes, I have two brothers. Now, if you take a look at this graph, it shows our first-year projections."

Morgan nodded, but he wasn't looking at the graph. Instead, he stared at me. I cleared my throat and presented the slides I'd prepared. He sat quietly, not interrupting me for the rest of the meeting. I went through thirty-two slides and not once did he ask a question. When I was done, I walked to my desk and brought the bottle of cognac I'd purchased. "What do you say we toast our new partnership?"

"I haven't agreed to anything yet, Crawford," he said.

I knew that. But he hadn't said no either. What else did I have to do to make this deal happen?

Morgan stood. "Well, I'll be in touch."

He wasn't going to sign the deal. I recognized his unimpressed look. I'd given it to others myself many times before. But I couldn't let him leave with that look on his face. I had to change his mind.

What would Frances do?

"Congratulations, once again, on your granddaughter's christening," I said, just as Morgan was about to step out of my office. As I'd hoped, he halted.

Pursing his lips, he turned around. "Thank you for the gift. My family appreciated the gesture."

Sensing he would walk out again, I blurted out what I wanted to say from the beginning. "Mr. Morgan, sir. I really need this property. I've been planning this development for nearly five years and this property is the last piece of the project."

"Why my property? Why not buy the one just north of me?"

"Because yours is next to the highway and we have all the permits in place."

"Well, it looks as though you may have counted your chickens before they hatched."

"I'll make you a partner," I said, formulating a new plan in my head. "If you sell me the property, I'll make you a five percent partner."

"Twenty-five percent," said Morgan.

Twenty-five percent was a large chunk, considering he'd done nothing up to this point. But if I wanted his property, this may be the only way.

"Fine," I said, then extended my hand. But Morgan didn't shake it.

"What are you doing this weekend?" he asked.

"Celebrating our new partnership?" I said with a grin.

Frowning, Morgan said, "My family and I will be heading to our cabin this weekend. Before I partner with anyone, I make sure my wife is on board. She is a great judge of character. If you can impress her by the end of the weekend, we have a deal."

All I had to do was impress a sweet little old lady? Piece of cake. A smile spread across my face. "Sounds great."

"I presume my office will communicate a lot with your assistant on daily matters?" Morgan asked.

"Yes, but you can always come directly to me if you prefer."

"I'm sure you're a busy man. But that means we will need to get to know her, too."

I glanced over Morgan's shoulder at Ava sitting at her desk, her hand under her chin, staring at her monitor. "I will check if she's available."

"Oh, not that one. I want you to bring the other assistant. I noticed the way you looked at her, Colton." He chuckled and patted my shoulder. "Don't worry. That's how I met my darling Marie."

What!

"Mr. Morgan," I began, but he stopped me.

"Is that going to be a problem, Crawford?"

I got the feeling the deal would be dead if I said yes.

"No, sir. Not a problem."

"Good. I'll have my assistant send you the directions. I hope you have a GPS. There are hardly any road signs in the area."

"Wonderful," I mumbled. But getting lost was the least of my concerns. I needed to face Frances and get her to agree to this trip.

14

Frances

On the bus ride back from work, I went over what I should've said to that customer who was rude to me earlier. Some great one-liners came to mind now, but an hour ago, I had stood there and I'd taken her abuse. I'd grown up with the saying, "the customer's always right". I believed it, too, until today.

Tired and cranky, I wanted only to curl up in bed and read a romance novel. But when I approached my house, a familiar car was parked in the driveway.

No. Not him. Not today.

As soon as I stepped inside, his voice seized my heart and I couldn't breathe. I closed my eyes and forced a few shaky breaths through my mouth.

"Frannie, is that you?" Marco called from the living room.

I ignored him.

"Frannie, come see who's here."

You can do this, Frances. You can talk to him.

I slowly slid my shoes off and turned the corner toward our living room. Next to my brother on the couch sat the man who had made my late teens and early twenties a nightmare. *Him.* My ex-boyfriend, Chris.

"Hey, Frannie," he said, rising from the couch. Instinctively, I took a step back and he frowned.

I hadn't seen Chris in three years, not since I'd caught him cheating and finally left him. He had tried calling to explain that the half-naked woman on his couch was just a friend, but I'd finally had enough of Chris. He didn't argue much about it after that call. It seemed like he'd found someone better.

"What are you doing here?" I asked, controlling the cadence of my voice. My family only knew we had broken up, nothing else.

"I came to see you, Frannie," he said, moving closer to me.

"Well, I don't want to see you," I said in a low voice and crossed my arms. I wanted to shield myself from him and how small he had made me feel.

Tilting his head toward my brother, Chris said, "Maybe we can go up to your room so we can talk in private."

I shook my head. Marco was eight years younger, but I still felt better having him next to me. I didn't trust Chris at all.

"Come on, baby," he said.

"Don't call me that," I whispered, and when he stepped closer to me, my lungs emptied. Pivoting toward the front door, I opened it, hoping to get some air. Instead, standing in front of me with his hand raised in a fist, prepared to knock, was Colton.

I sucked in a deep breath and covered my mouth. "What are *you* doing here?"

"We need to talk, Frances," he said. "May I come in?"

"Who's this guy?" asked Chris in a hard voice, coming up behind me. His anger had the usual effect, and a wave of nausea overtook me for a second.

"Are you all right?" asked Colton, watching me carefully.

"I'm fine," I said. Then, closing my eyes and hardening my voice, I added, "Chris, I want you to leave. Now." I opened the door wider and stood behind it. Colton didn't move. His eyes assessed Chris and they narrowed.

"Who is this, Frances?" asked Colton.

"None of your concern," I said.

"Who the *fuck* are you?" snarled Chris.

Colton stepped inside and looked down at Chris. He was taller by at least three inches. "She asked you to leave. I suggest you go before I show you out myself. And I don't ask as nicely as she does."

Chris measured Colton, his eyes scanning his body, and must have figured he'd lose this fight. Despite his bravado, Chris had always been a coward.

Putting his hand on my waist, Chris whispered close to my ear, "I'll see you soon, Frannie," and shoved Colton on his way out the door.

Waiting for the wave of nausea to waft through me, I exhaled a sigh of relief when his beat-up truck finally pulled out of my driveway. Colton stared after him as well and didn't face me until we could no longer see the vehicle.

"Want to tell me what that was about?" he asked.

"Not really," I said. "What do you want, Colton?" Because I didn't have the energy to deal with him right now. My body drained of its adrenaline, I just wanted to curl up and sleep.

"We need to talk. I need a few minutes of your time. You owe me that."

Exhausted, I responded, holding nothing back. "I owed you an explanation weeks ago but you didn't care to hear one."

"Fine. How about giving me ten minutes of your time for not calling the police and reporting you for identity fraud?"

I narrowed my eyes at him. "You really are a jerk, you know that?" But I moved out of the doorway and let him inside.

"Frannie, do you want me to stay?" asked Marco, standing in the hallway.

"No. But thank you."

Marco stared at Colton for another minute. "I'll just be in the kitchen if you need me."

I nodded, and we both watched Marco walk away. My heartbeat slowed, but my thoughts raced.

Why would Chris come back here after all these years?

I would think about that later. Right now, I had to worry about Colton, and being near him threatened to start my heart back up again—only this time for a different reason.

I sat down on the couch and crossed my legs, waiting for Colton to reveal why he'd shown up at my doorstep unexpectedly. He paced the living room instead.

"I had a meeting with Robert Morgan today," he said, finally. "It didn't go well. He didn't sign the papers."

"Did you buy his favorite bottle of cognac?"

A small grin played on his lips. "I did."

I nodded, a bit impressed he had considered it. I recalled all the research we'd come up with independently and together, and asked, "Did you show him all the graphs we'd prepared and the projections?"

"I showed him everything. But he wants more."

"What else could he want?"

"You."

"Me?" I sat back, surprised by his answer.

"When I realized Morgan wasn't going to sign the deal today, I panicked and offered to make him a five percent partner."

I snorted. "He would never agree to anything less than twenty percent."

"You're right. He asked for twenty-five."

Wrapping my arms around my knees, as I still felt shaken having seen Chris again, I said, "Well, if you really want this to happen, you'll have to accept it."

"I did. But there's one more condition. Morgan said he doesn't partner with anyone until his wife gives him her approval."

"You shouldn't have a problem. You can be charming when you put your mind to it. As long as they aren't one of your employees."

He steepled his fingers in front of him and turned toward me. "He wants her to meet my assistant as well."

"Then you should ask—" Then it hit me. "He thinks that I'm still your assistant?"

"I may have said something about you only being on a temporary leave of absence."

I raised my eyebrows at him. "So, you lied?"

"I wouldn't call it a lie."

"I would."

"This wasn't the same thing, Frances. I didn't sleep with the guy."

His words hit me in the chest, as he had to have known they would. I closed my eyes, deciding what I would do. On the one hand, I could use this as an opportunity to make amends for my actions, but on the other, I would just be a puppet in someone else's charade. I hated lying in the first place and didn't wish to lie to Morgan and his family. Not even for Colton. I was tired. This week, especially this day, had taken a lot out of me, but for the first time in a long time, I didn't want to sacrifice myself to please others. I would choose what was best for me.

"No," I said.

"No?"

I nodded and he stared back at me, surprised.

I enjoyed the moment until he opened his mouth again. "I'll pay you for the two weeks you worked as my assistant."

"You should have paid me for those two weeks in the first place."

"I will now. I'll tell Frank in HR to pay you," he said. Then, putting his hands on his hips, he asked, "How did he not pick up on the same social security number that was already on file?"

Oh boy. "I may have told him I'd lost my card and was waiting for my new number to come in."

He shook his head. "Lying comes quite easily to you, doesn't it?"

"Not usually," I admitted. "But I needed the money."

I still did. We didn't have enough saved up yet for Marco's first semester, but I had one more idea of how we'd pay for it without lying for Colton. I would look into it tomorrow. I wasn't desperate yet.

"I'm sorry, Colton. But my answer is still no."

I braced myself for the angry outburst, the name-calling, the sulking I usually received from Chris when I denied him what he wanted. But Colton stayed pensive. He stopped pacing and sat next to me on the couch.

"Why did you do it, Frances?" he asked, staring straight ahead, his elbows on his knees, his chin resting on his folded hands.

"We needed money to pay for Marco's—"

"No. Not that. Why did you sleep with me?"

That question was more difficult to answer. But I would give him the truth. "I've wanted to sleep with you from the moment I first saw you."

He smiled. "Me too. I wanted to rip that notebook from your hands and lay you on my desk."

"That wasn't the first time I saw you. I've had a crush on you for years, Colton. Despite the entire office hating you, I never did."

"The entire office hates me?" he asked, swinging his face to look at me. "Even the mailroom?"

I scoffed. "You must know that you're arrogant, rude, and short with them."

His furrowed brow and his incredulous face should have made me laugh, but it angered me instead. "You don't see your employees for who they are, only what they can do for you. I worked at your company for years, Colton. I stood on the twelfth floor next to

Erika as you walked to the elevators hundreds of times and yet you didn't care who I was until I stood in your office, resume in hand, and a spot to fill in your busy day."

He pressed his lips together and nodded. "You're right. But that doesn't change the fact that you lied. My arrogance may have opened the door but you walked right in."

"I did," I said, without hesitation. "But you also never gave me a chance to explain when everything blew up in your office."

His jaw clenched and he turned his body on the couch to look at me. His eyes fell to my lips. I recognized the look. It made my stomach clench, my body wanting what my heart refused to say. He opened his mouth to speak, but quickly shut it.

I waited for him to ask me if I was still attracted to him. I prayed that he wouldn't because the answer was still yes. But what did it matter? There was so much deception between us, even though my feelings for him were real. How could he ever trust me? And would I spend years trying to make it up to him? It didn't sound like a healthy relationship to me. It was best that Colton and I moved on from this entire ordeal.

"You will be fine with the Morgans," I said. "When you put your mind to it, you can be as charming as Luke and as shrewd as Ryan."

His cheeks twitched in a semblance of a smile. His eyes crinkled at the sides. Then he stood and put his hand out to help me up from the couch. "I wish things had gone down differently, Frances. I think we could have been good together."

"Me too, Colton." *Me too.*

I walked him to the door, and when he turned, extending his hand, I gave up. I threw myself into his arms, and he held me tightly against him. "Goodbye, Colton. And good luck."

"Goodbye, Frances."

He cleared his throat and walked to his car, not looking back. I watched his car pull onto the street until my watery eyes couldn't see straight anymore. Then I finally went upstairs, curled up in my bed, and wished I'd never fallen in love with Colton Crawford.

Despite my sadness, my heart warned me that this wasn't over.

15

Frances

The next day was Saturday and I started my shift at the store at eleven o'clock. I still had one hour to put my other plan into motion. Rummaging through my top drawer, my fingers brushed up against a plush velvet jewelry box.

Lifting the lid off the hinge, I pulled out the eighteen-karat gold necklace with a round pendant. Etched on the pendant was the figure of Mother Mary holding baby Jesus in her arms. My grandmother had given me the necklace on my First Communion day. I had only ever worn it on special occasions, along with the gold bracelet my parents had gifted me. I grabbed the white box that held the bracelet and hid both in my purse.

Running down the stairs, I glimpsed my *Nonna* in the kitchen frying bacon. I didn't want to stop and talk with her this morning; I was too afraid I'd change my mind.

"I'm off to work," I said, slipping on my jacket.

"See you later, *bella*," she said. "I'll prepare your favorite for dinner. Agnolotti with ricotta and spinach."

I groaned from the hallway. How did she manage to make me feel guilty without even knowing what I was about to do? I swore my grandmother had a sixth sense of knowing whenever Marco and

I would get ourselves into trouble even before we came up with our silly plan. Only my plan wasn't silly, it was heartbreaking, but necessary under the circumstances.

I raced outside and down the street. The pawnshop was just in front of my usual bus stop, but I'd never been inside. I didn't own anything of much value and had never been tempted to sell my gold until now. A pang of regret struck me, but I reminded myself I was doing this for my family, not myself.

A bell chimed at the door when I stepped inside. A man with black hair and a handlebar mustache stood behind a glass counter. He was polishing some silver spoons when he asked, "What can I do for you, miss?"

I approached the counter and noticed the jewelry encased. There were rings, bracelets, necklaces, and more. Some pieces were small and one, in particular, was quite extravagant. "Wow, that one's gorgeous," I said, pointing to the thick gold necklace with an enormous emerald in the center.

He opened the glass in front to pull out the necklace. "Oh no, I'm not here to buy. I'm looking to sell," I said.

"Oh, in that case, show me what you've got," he said, sliding the glass door shut.

Pulling the two boxes from my purse, I opened them for his inspection. From his front shirt pocket, he pulled out a pair of glasses and held the pendant in his hand. "Eighteen karats, that's good," he murmured, turning the piece over. He did the same to the bracelet.

Putting down his eyeglasses onto the counter, he said, "I'll give you two hundred for both."

"What? They're worth more than that. Gold is at a premium these days," I argued.

He sucked his top teeth and shook his head. "The religious images don't sell too well. I'll have to melt them down. That's my best offer."

Two hundred wouldn't be enough to pay for Marco's first semester. We'd be short and I'd have sold my jewelry for nothing.

"Thank you, but I won't sell them for that price."

"No problem," he said, returning to his silver. "When you change your mind, you know where to find me."

The nerve! "You know, profiting from someone's desperation is a crappy way to make a living," I said.

He put down the spoon and tilted his head. "Well, show me a business that doesn't profit from desperation. Besides, I'm not forcing anyone to do anything."

I shook my head and left the pawnshop feeling worse than when I thought I'd sell my family's gifts. *Now what?*

I thought back to Colton sitting on my couch yesterday. I had called him proud, but now my pride could cost Marco his dream. *Don't panic, Frances.* I still had other options.

While waiting for the bus, I decided I would ask my manager, Cheryl, for some extra shifts at work. I didn't think it would be enough, but it would be a start.

My stomach knotted at the thought of approaching her. It seemed ridiculous, but I recalled the words my parents would often say to us, 'never demand things in life; if you deserve them they will come'. Or 'you will be rewarded for your loyalty to a company if you work hard and show your commitment'.

Hmm. I wonder if this is where some of my resistance to confrontation began?

There was no time to dwell on that thought, nor anytime to wait for the company to reward my loyalty. I needed the extra money now.

When I arrived at work, Cheryl didn't greet me as usual. Instead, she shifted her eyes in my direction, then looked away. It wasn't very encouraging, as I already felt nervous asking her for extra hours.

"Cheryl, do you have a moment to speak before my shift begins?"

I asked, approaching her as she keyed something into the cash register.

"If it's about your hours, we had to make some adjustments," she said while staring at the computer screen.

How did she know I wanted to talk about my hours? "What do you mean?"

"Lin's been killing it on the floor, so when she asked for more hours, I gave them to her."

"But I've been here longer than Lin," I said, feeling my voice crack. I would not cry in front of Cheryl. "Don't I at least get first dibs on more shifts?"

"That's not how it works, Frances. I don't owe you anything. Sorry," she said and shrugged her shoulders, not sounding sorry at all.

Indignation crawled up my throat, scratching to get out, but I swallowed it down. "I need those hours," I said.

"Well, sell more clothes and you'll get them." She still hadn't looked at me since I walked up to her. From the stubborn set of her jaw, I could see that nothing I could say would change her mind. Panic replaced my anger and I felt on the brink of hyperventilating.

I turned and walked to the backroom. Dropping my head into my hands, I inhaled a few deep breaths, exhaling slowly through my nose, hoping to bring my emotions under control, but it was no use.

Dammit! That's not how this was supposed to go.

I wasn't upset that I'd lost the shifts to Lin. I wasn't even upset that I sucked at this job. I was desperate and angry that every time I tried to open a new door, it slammed shut in my face. It was as though the universe conspired against me. *What do I do now?* I tried everything. I used up all my options. I tried every door.

Except for one.

That door I'd closed myself. But I had shut it for a reason. I couldn't work for Colton again, not even for pretend this time. My feelings were too real and I knew I'd get hurt. He didn't want to rekindle a romance with me. He just wanted someone to help him seal the Morgan deal. That was it.

Pull up your big girl socks, Frances, and get up.

If he could disconnect his feelings for business, well, so could I. I was tired of waiting for life to happen. What if my parents were wrong? I wanted to make things happen for me.

I would use this opportunity to ask for something I needed from Colton. Cheryl was right; I hated this job. But I'd loved the PA position. I would apply for another one at a different company, this time as Frances Netto. But I needed something from Colton first.

I hit Colton's number on my phone before I could lose my nerve.

"Hello," he answered.

"Hi, it's me," I said.

"Frances, is everything all right?"

"I'll come with you to Morgan's cabin," I said.

He was silent on the other end. I wasn't sure if he was celebrating or cursing.

"That's great," he said calmly, his voice giving nothing away. "What changed your mind?"

"Circumstances," I said.

"I leave in an hour. Is that enough time for you to be ready?"

"Yes," I answered. "But I need something from you."

"What's that?"

"A reference letter."

Silence again. Then, "You plan on applying for another PA position?"

"Yes."

"Fine. Be ready in an hour," he said and hung up the phone.

Rising from the steel chair on a big exhale, I walked to the bathroom and splashed water onto my face. Staring in the mirror, I gave myself one last pep talk before I spoke to Cheryl. *You got this,*

Frances. I'd never quit anything before, but oddly, this didn't feel like quitting. It felt like living.

Straightening my gray blazer, I walked up to Cheryl. "I'm leaving," I said.

"Where do you think you're going?" she asked with a hand on her hip.

"I quit," I said.

"You owe me two weeks' notice," she called after me.

Without bothering to turn around, I shouted back, "Like you said, Cheryl, I don't owe you anything."

***

Exactly one hour later, Colton's car pulled into my driveway. Somehow, I'd showered and packed a bag in that short amount of time.

"Francesca, there's someone at the door for you," my grandmother shouted. I smiled, recalling Colton's security system versus mine. *Nonna* must have spotted the car while sitting in the living room watching *Wheel of Fortune*. I didn't understand how she loved that show so much when she never once guessed the phrase correctly.

"Coming," I said, and heaved the overnight bag over my shoulder.

"Is that Colton's car?" asked Marco as I walked past the bathroom.

"Yes."

"I thought that was over," he said.

"It is."

"It doesn't seem over to him."

"It's not what you think. It's complicated." I tried to move past him, but he stopped me with a hand on my shoulder. "Try me."

Adjusting the strap, I said, "A client specifically asked for me. Colton needs me to show up at this man's cabin to get this deal done."

"And what do you get?" he asked, crossing his arms over his chest.

"I get my two weeks' pay and a reference letter."

"Sounds like he's getting a lot more out of this arrangement."

"Look, Marco. I appreciate your concern, I do. But I can take care of myself."

As soon as the words left my mouth, the truth behind them straightened my spine. I'd never given myself credit for walking out on Chris. I may have allowed him to yell at me and call me names, but I'd left him. No one had rescued me. I had to rely on myself to get out of that situation. For the last few years, I hadn't permitted myself to be proud of myself. Focusing instead, on all the things I'd done wrong, like how I'd stayed for too long.

But I'd never given myself credit for leaving. If I'd shut myself off from the rest of the world, since meeting Chris, hoping no one would see me for the mess I thought I was, I now felt like I'd opened the door—just a little bit. Perhaps it was enough to let the old me back out.

"Be careful," he shouted as I ran down the stairs. My mom would shout this to us every time she heard us running to the steps and we always quipped back the same response.

"Holding onto the railing, mom," I said, chuckling.

He popped his head over the balustrade. "I meant to be careful with your heart."

Caught by surprise, I looked up to catch his gaze. The concern on his face tightened my chest. "I will," I said and walked out the door.

Colton stood next to his car, wearing a pair of blue jeans and a white cashmere sweater. I hated the way my heart did a little somersault against my ribcage whenever I saw him.

"Hi," I said, keeping my eyes away from his face.

He cleared his throat. "Hi."

Colton reached forward and lifted my bag from my shoulder and carried it to his car. When I sat in the front seat and turned to him, I set the ground rules.

"This is purely business. Two days, one night, and then I get what I want and you get your signature."

"Right," said Colton, looking at me with a furrowed brow. "Except there's just one more thing."

I prepared myself for his version of the 'it's only business' speech. "What is it?" I asked.

"Morgan thinks that we're in love."

"He... *what*?" I shouted, not expecting those words at all.

"He insinuated it... I think." Colton rubbed his creased forehead. "I don't recall his exact words, but you don't need to worry. We won't be showing any public display of affection."

"Good," I said, but why then did I feel sad about it? It was confusing sitting in a car with Colton, pretending to be his girlfriend after he fired me for pretending to be Ava Grady. Everything was so messed up. I didn't know what was happening, but I would figure it all out after this weekend. I just had to get through the next forty-eight hours.

16

Colton

This was harder than I thought it would be. I'd prepared my own ground rules before arriving at Frances's house. But she beat me to it. Except after seeing her, all I wanted to do was break those rules and kiss that mouth. But she was right. There was too much between us. Despite the explosive chemistry, I still couldn't trust her. She'd lied to me, had pretended to be someone else.

Would she be honest with me moving forward?

"Who was that guy yesterday?" I asked, hoping she would tell me the truth. I suspected it was her ex-boyfriend, but I didn't understand why he was there.

She stared straight ahead and didn't answer, fidgeting with her fingers on her lap.

"Blonde guy," I continued. "The one with the big mouth and small balls."

"Yes. I know whom you were referring to. I just don't want to talk about it."

I pressed down on my lips. She wasn't lying, just avoiding the truth.

"How far is the cabin from here?" she asked.

"About an hour and a half drive," I said, checking my app.

Looking out her passenger window, she added, "I'm going to close my eyes for a bit until we get there."

"Didn't you sleep last night?" I asked.

Why isn't she sleeping? Did the asshole say something to upset her?

"Not really. Got a lot on my mind right now."

My first instinct was to reach over and run my hand down her hair and rub her back, but I clenched the steering wheel instead. Frances Netto's worries were not my concern.

Only a few minutes had passed when light breathing hummed from the other side of the car. I avoided any potholes on the road and turned down the radio.

Driving down country lanes reminded me of when my brothers and I would take road trips with my parents. My dad, who loved the outdoors, would take us camping, fishing, and hiking nearly every weekend. We didn't have a cabin, but I suspected it was only because my father didn't want to be tied to one place. My brothers and I have never been camping since. I said it was because I didn't have time, but I knew it wouldn't be the same without my father.

Following the app's instructions, I turned onto a dirt road. Tall log trees lined the gravel driveway, reminding me of tall sentinels standing guard. A wood-faced cabin with a gray roof and a white wrap-around porch sat in the middle of an open field. They had built a barn house next to it and a coral right in front. I didn't see any horses, but suspected they were in the barn.

Pulling up to the front of the cabin, a large golden retriever ran over to greet us. His enthusiastic barking woke Frances. Moaning in her seat, she pushed herself up and rubbed her eyes. The sound made me groan inwardly.

"Did I sleep through the entire car ride?"

"You did," I said, watching her straighten the neckline of her sweater that had fallen off her shoulder while she'd slept.

Staring out the window, her eyes soaked in the sight in front of us. I'd forgotten how majestic the forest could be until the sparkle in Frances's eyes reminded me.

"Have you ever been this far north?" I asked.

"Never," she whispered. "It's beautiful here."

Staring at her mouth, slightly opened in awe, I had to agree. "It certainly is."

"There's Morgan," said Frances, pointing to a figure emerging from the trees. Robert Morgan wore brown pants and a red and black checkered shirt. A brown felt hat sat on his head with a white feather sticking out. He looked ridiculous, but somehow not unexpected for Morgan. Another man accompanied him, but from this distance, I didn't recognize him.

Stepping out of the car, the dog nearly bowled Frances over, pawing at her thighs. "Hi, buddy," she cooed. Then, looking up at the two men approaching us, she shouted, "Is this Taylor?"

"Sure is," Morgan shouted back as Frances crouched and gave the dog a proper rub-down—belly rub and all. The little beast licked her hands in appreciation.

As Morgan and his companion approached the car, I kept my gaze on the second man until his features became clearer. He had dark blonde hair, about my height, and nearly the same build. As he walked closer, the shape of his eyes reminded me of Morgan's. This had to be his son.

"Welcome," Morgan said when he finally reached us.

"Thank you for having me." Frances wiped her hands on her jeans and shook hands with both men. Not liking the appreciative look the younger man aimed at Frances, I introduced myself.

"Colton Crawford," I said, and may have squeezed the man's hand harder than necessary.

"Paul Morgan," he said, narrowing his eyes and clasping his fingers tighter around mine.

"Paul, this is the man I was telling you about," said his father.

Then his lips curved up into a smile and he added, "And this is his assistant, Frances." He beamed at her, likely proud that he remembered her name this time.

Paul turned to give Frances a big-tooth smile. "It's a pleasure to meet you." His thumb swept across her hand as he shook it. I wanted to pull that thumb back until I heard it snap. Frances smiled back, unaware of my possessive thoughts.

"Come inside and meet the rest of the family." We followed Morgan as his boots clomped up the porch. The crackling of a fire welcomed us as we entered the cabin. Mounted on either side of the stone fireplace were two moose heads with the largest antlers I'd ever seen.

"You must be Colton," said a woman, coming down the stairs.

She looked to be Morgan's age, in her early sixties, with white hair pulled back into a bun. Her full, rosy cheeks reminded me of some wholesome baking commercial. "Yes, ma'am," I said, extending my hand. "This is my… assistant, Frances." Frances turned to me with a question in her eyes, before redirecting her attention to the woman.

"You have a lovely cabin, Mrs. Morgan," she said. "Did you design the interior yourself?"

"Please, you must both call me Marie. And oh, no," she chuckled. "I'd never put those awful antlers up there if it were up to me. But marriage takes compromise, dear," she said, and winked at Frances. Then, pointing to the staircase she'd just descended, she said, "Paul, why don't you show Frances to her room and take her bags?"

Paul picked up the bags I'd left at the front door and gave Frances a half-smile, allowing only one side of his lips to curl up. I used that smile, too, when I wanted to show a woman I was interested in her.

"I can take them," I said, grabbing one of the bags from Paul's hand, but he didn't let go.

"Nonsense," said Robert. "Let me show you my hunting collection."

I'd rather pop my eye out with one of those antlers, I thought. But I released the bag and watched Paul escort Frances upstairs, leading her to one of the bedrooms. Not wanting to make it obvious I was staring, I turned back to Robert. But he gave a knowing look to his wife, who smirked up at the staircase. "Didn't I tell you?" he mumbled under his breath, but I'd heard him. "I think he likes her."

Is he talking about me or his son?

Now I wasn't sure if Morgan was trying to nurture what he thought was a burgeoning relationship between me and Frances, or start one for his son? I wasn't one to beat around the bush. "Robert, did you invite me here so you could set up my assistant with your son?"

"Nonsense," he said, but I didn't believe him. When I held his stare with my arms crossed, he shrugged his shoulders. "You've got nothing to worry about, right, Crawford? You can handle a bit of competition."

Annoyed, I inhaled a loud breath and exhaled sharply.

Marie put her hand on her hip. "Nothing's going on between you and your assistant, is there, Colton? That wouldn't be very professional." She laughed, then winked. Was she teasing me or warning me? I got the feeling Marie was the sort of mother that used the same passive-aggressive tone to get what she wanted.

"There's nothing untoward happening, ma'am. I assure you," I said, careful not to admit to anything unprofessional, but still not denying any relationship with Frances.

"Good. Then let's start with my knife collection," said Morgan. "I got a beauty the other day that would skin a fish in ten seconds flat."

"Great," I deadpanned.

Morgan laughed and put his arm around my shoulder. If I wasn't imagining Frances with another man upstairs, I might have enjoyed the camaraderie with him.

17

Frances

The carpeted staircase led to a narrow hallway upstairs. Family pictures lined the wood-paneled walls. A photo of a little boy chasing an older girl in the backyard caught my attention, reminding me of myself and Marco.

"That's my sister, Natalie," said Paul, standing behind me.

"The age gap looks similar to that of me and my brother. We're eight years apart." I walked to the next photo, this one of Mr. Morgan carrying Paul on his shoulders.

"We're seven years apart, but she acts like it's seventeen," said Paul in a dry voice.

I chuckled. "Yes, well, we older sisters are a lot more mature, so it might as well be seventeen."

"Is that right?" he asked. While I couldn't see his face, I could hear the grin in his voice as he stepped in closer behind me. I wasn't sure if the woodsy scent was his cologne or him, but it smelled nice. Pointing to the room next to me, I cleared my throat and asked, "Is this one mine?"

"Yes." He stepped into the room and shoved his hands in his pockets. "Will it work for you?"

A queen-size bed with a cream-colored comforter sat in the

middle of the room. Two nightstands flanked the bed with a trunk at its foot and a dresser in front.

I snorted softly. "Yup. This will work." It was larger than my parents's bedroom at home.

Paul opened the lid to the trunk and pulled out a wool blanket. "In case you get cold, here's an extra one."

"That's thoughtful of you," I said.

He smiled, then looked down at my clothes. "Do you need a few minutes to change, or are you comfortable in jeans?"

"Change for what?"

He grinned as though he was about to share a childhood secret. "Morgan family tradition."

When I raised my eyebrows in anticipation, he added, "Family football."

"Oh cool," I said, not really excited about watching football. "Who's playing?"

"You are."

"I am?" I blurted out, horrified.

If possible, his boyish grin grew wider and he chuckled at my response. "We always kick off the weekend with a friendly football game. Losers make the winners breakfast the next morning."

"I don't know the first thing about football," I said, shaking my head.

"That's okay." He crossed his arms over his tight-fitting blue sweater. "I'll teach you."

My first instinct was to say 'no'. I would find some excuse and watch the game from the porch. But I made a deal to help Colton, and bowing out of Morgan's first request would not be a good start. So, I pushed my anxious thoughts from my mind and raised my chin. "Looking forward to it."

Paul playfully punched me on the shoulder before jogging out of the room. Rubbing the spot, I groaned. *This should be interesting.*

***

When I stepped onto the wide front lawn, everyone was already outside, tossing the football around. To say I was intimidated was an understatement. I wasn't worried about breaking a nail. I was worried about breaking a limb.

"Colton, since you and Frances are our guests, we'll let you choose your teammate," said Robert.

Colton's gaze fell directly on me, and without looking at anyone else, he said, "I'll take Frances." The deep timber in his voice made me shiver. I hated how he still had that effect on me.

Paul nodded. "Smart man."

"Don't worry, son," said Robert. "We can take'em."

As father and son high-fived each other, I asked, "What about you, Marie? Whose team are you on?"

"I'm the referee," she said, pulling out a whistle from her back pocket. Paul wasn't kidding when he said they took their family football game seriously.

Marie blew her whistle twice and shouted, "All right, people, line up!"

I whipped my head from side to side, looking at where I should stand. Colton came up behind me and placed his hand on my shoulder. "Do you know how to play?" he asked.

"Not really," I admitted. "I only ever watch the half-time show at The Superbowl."

He shook his head. "Okay. You're going to turn around and face Robert. I'll take Paul. He's going to throw the football to Robert. Your job is to intercept the pass or take the football away from him if he catches it."

"I can't do that to an old man," I said.

"Well, you don't have to take the guy down, Frances. Just try to take the ball away from him."

"All right, I'll try."

Marie blew the whistle again. "Ready?"

Colton guided me into position with a steady hand on my lower back. I bit my lip, holding back a sigh at the familiar gesture.

Robert held the football between his ankles and snapped it to Paul behind him, just as Colton had said he would. I glued myself to Robert's side and waved my hands in front of him. Meanwhile, Colton ran like a tiger toward Paul and rammed a shoulder into him, throwing Paul off balance. But Paul still managed to toss the football toward his father. I jumped up to catch it but missed. The ball landed in Robert's hands and he took off faster than I'd seen any white-haired man run.

"Touch down!" he shouted when he reached the makeshift end zone.

"I'm sorry," I said to Colton when we met back up at the scrimmage line.

"Don't worry about it," he said, his hand squeezing my shoulder. "You were close. Okay, we're up next."

I nodded but had no idea what that meant.

"You're going to toss the ball toward me, just like Robert did," he explained.

"Okay."

"I want you to run like hell toward our end zone. Once you pass that tree, turn around and wait for me to throw you the football. Got it?"

"Got it," I said, rubbing my hands together.

I grabbed the football from Colton and placed it on the ground, just like Robert had done. Bending over and looking for Colton behind me, I spotted a smile playing on his lips.

"What?"

"You know. We should have played football in Miami. This is giving me all sorts of ideas."

The heat in his eyes made me blush and warmed other areas of my body, too.

"Stop it," I mouthed back at him. "They can hear you."

"White 80!" he shouted, and I turned around.

"What?"

"It just means we're ready. Get into position."

I didn't know why those words made my face flush, but I quickly put my head down between my legs. Colton extended his hands, waiting for the football, while I closed my eyes and hiked it toward him. Miraculously, he caught it.

"Run!" he shouted, and I did.

I ran as fast as I could toward the tree, arms pumping on either side of me. The tree was less than a foot away when harsh breaths caught up to me, and then two hands grabbed me from the waist and pulled me back.

I froze.

I knew it was Paul holding me tightly against his body, but the feeling of being held down terrified me. The blood drained from my body and I shivered from the cold. My eyes were open, but I saw nothing in front of me except a fuzzy blue haze.

Someone called my name. It was Colton. He sounded panicked. I forced my eyes to focus and slowly Colton's familiar figure became clearer. He was far away, but I could distinguish his shape and then his face. In the next moment, his eyes rounded to the size of footballs.

Running toward Colton, roaring with his arms outstretched, was Robert. Although he was shorter than Colton, the man had momentum on his side, and Colton was unprepared for the unstoppable train coming straight at him. Robert barreled into Colton, sending both men flying into the air, and then Colton landed hard on his back.

Paul let go of me to whoop and celebrate his father's tackle. I briefly closed my eyes and waited for the adrenaline to slow down and my fears to subside. When I opened them, the two men were still on the ground. Having broken his fall on Colton's prone body, Robert stood first.

"You okay there, Colton?" he asked, extending his hand.

Colton took it, lifting himself off the ground.

"Good game," said Colton. "But I think Frances and I are done for the day." He dusted his jeans as he walked up to me.

Robert laughed and called out, "Now you know what you're getting yourself into, Crawford." Colton seemed to ignore him, walking straight toward me.

"You okay?" he asked in a low voice. "Your face went pale and blank when Paul grabbed you."

I nodded. "I'm okay." I meant it too. Now that I was free from Paul's tight grip, I could breathe normally. I also recalled Colton's face right before Robert tackled him. "Are you all right?" I asked.

Colton shook his head but laughed. "I should have known he was one tough son of a bitch. I shouldn't have underestimated him."

"It's not your fault. People often allow you to see only what they want you to see," I said, thinking how many times I'd hidden from the world.

Colton looked pensive, his eyes unfocused. "Yes. And I seemed to get fooled every time."

Guilt chewed my insides. But when I looked up at him again, he wasn't staring at me. No accusatory glare or even a sad little smile. His face remained hard, and he looked toward the treetops. Then, I finally understood. Someone else had hurt him before.

"Do you want to talk about it?" I asked.

My question brought his gaze to my face, and he gave me that sad smile I'd looked for earlier. "Do you want to talk about what happened in your past?"

Huh. He got me there. "No."

"That's what I thought." Dusting the dirt off his sweater, Colton straightened and stared at the cloudy sky. "Guess neither of us is ready to be honest with each other yet."

He was right. I wasn't ready to talk about it, and it sounded like neither was he. That left us at an impasse. How could we move past what happened at work if we weren't willing to trust each other with our secrets?

I hadn't expected Colton to say that, but I was glad of it. We'd both admitted we were keeping secrets from one another and that felt like the most honest we'd been since I'd walked into his office. At least with our clothes on. I smiled at the memory.

I'd never been closer to anyone than I'd been that night in Miami with Colton. But then my walls went up the next day, and while they still hadn't come down, perhaps there was a window now and I could see into Colton's heart a little clearer. Someone he loved and trusted had hurt him. I could feel it in my own heart.

"What are you smiling about?" he asked when we reached the porch stairs.

"Just that I think I understand you a little better now," I said, waiting on the bottom step.

He rested his arm on the railing. "You do?"

I nodded and smiled. "What do you think the Morgans have planned next for us?"

Colton groaned and he rubbed his forehead. "I have no idea, but I'm a little nervous to find out." I laughed at the mock horror on his face.

"What's so funny?" asked Paul, a small smirk on his lips.

"Colton's face," I said, and giggled.

"Is that so?" said Colton, crossing his arms. I wasn't intimidated. His lips twitched and I knew he held back a laugh.

"Yep," I teased.

Paul stared at us before asking, "How about we slow down the pace and take a walk by the lake, Frances?" He was looking at me, but Colton answered instead.

"That's a great idea, Paul. I'll just grab my jacket."

Paul sighed. "Wonderful."

This time, I was the one to hold back my laugh, as neither man looked happy about it.

***

Colton, Robert, and I followed Paul down a grassy path. It wasn't quite a road, but there were tire marks. Paul must have caught my gaze. "Those are from the ATVs. My brother-in-law and I often ride them when we're up here. I can take you for a ride later if you'd like," said Paul.

The conversation behind us ceased as though Colton awaited my response. "Thank you, but I will pass." I turned to him with a wry smile. "I'm not the thrill-seeker type."

As we walked past a small thatch of trees, I caught my first view of the serene lake. Not even a ripple passed through the water, making it look like a sheet of greyish blue glass. There was a wooden dock and two boats parked on either side.

Paul turned to me. "Well, it's too cold to swim, but the water isn't frozen yet. How about we go for a ride?"

"What do you say, Colton? You up for a ride?" asked Robert.

Colton glanced at me, perhaps searching for my reaction. Boating wasn't my thing either, but I didn't see the harm in it. I liked that I was exploring new activities and, strangely, I was less nervous than I'd been even just a few months ago. It was time I stopped holding myself back. "That sounds like a great idea," I said, and walked with Paul toward the boat.

"Fantastic, let's get in," said Robert, and Colton followed him.

Paul held my hand gently as he helped me into the boat. As it rocked from side to side, so did my stomach. My legs wobbled as I stepped closer to one of the seats and slowly lowered myself next to Paul at the front. I didn't think my stomach could handle the back. Colton and Robert took seats behind us.

"Robert, I was hoping to speak to you before dinner," Colton began, but Robert cut him off.

"Not now, Colton. There's plenty of time for business later."

The response unsettled me. I knew Robert had invited Colton to his cabin, but it seemed that it had nothing to do with business. It frustrated me, and I could only imagine how much it must frustrate Colton. We'd worked hard on those presentations. The least Robert could do was to hear him out.

"Would you like to drive the boat, Frances?" asked Paul.

"No, thank you," I said. "Considering I've never been on a boat before, it's best if you stick to the driving."

Paul laughed, but I wasn't trying to be funny.

"Colton, before I forget, my assistant Diane asked me to say hello," said Robert, and nudged Colton's arm with his elbow. "I get the feeling she knows you—how should I say it—quite intimately." He snickered.

"Diane and I had gone out before, but there's nothing between us now," Colton explained, looking at me, then back at Robert. I spun around to face the front of the boat. Colton's past or current relationships were no longer my concern.

"Well, it's not me you've got to convince, boy," said Robert with a guffaw. "It's the lady."

"Speaking of Diane," said Colton. "Did she give you the latest presentation? The one with the valet parking garage?"

Robert's laugh died on the spot, and he cleared his throat. "I don't recall at the moment."

"I'll be happy to go over it with you when we get back to the house."

I hid my smile with the back of my hand. Colton's quick wit shut Robert up immediately.

I stared across the lake, ignoring Robert's grumbling behind me. There were other cabins nestled on the other side of the water, some spanning at least fifty feet. It was a completely different world than the one I lived in. I thought of my family and how my grandmother would hate it here. She'd say she had left the wilderness of her home country so her family could realize their dreams in the city. 'Why should I fight mosquitoes all week long?' she'd told us when we suggested renting a cabin last summer. She'd said to save our money for Disney World instead. That was her idea of a vacation. The thought made me smile and I wrapped my arms around myself as a sudden breeze blew through my coat.

"Are you cold?" asked Colton.

"A little," I said.

"We should go back inside," suggested Colton as he unzipped his jacket. When he stood to remove it, Paul looked back and accidentally moved the steering wheel toward another property's dock.

"Careful!" I shouted. Paul yanked the steering wheel to the right and I crashed up against the side of the boat. Colton unfortunately did not. He teetered until his arms flailed like a windmill and he crashed into the dark water.

"Colton," I screamed, turning behind me and reaching for him. Colton broke the surface, his dark hair slicked back. His face wasn't angry, just startled. Paul and Robert reached for him and pulled him back inside the boat. He stood in a puddle in his black boots and jeans. Pieces of his black hair fell toward his face, and he pushed them back. He panted, his chest heaving, making him look like some sea god—about to exact his revenge. Instead, he said, "This boat ride is over."

Paul nodded and turned the boat around as Colton held onto the railing beside him. I stared ahead, not daring to turn around. I felt terrible for Colton, but I struggled to fight back a giggle. I was one of those people that laughed at the most inappropriate times to relieve my anxiety. So, I held my breath and chewed the inside of my cheek. Tears burned behind my eyes, but I didn't laugh.

"Well, Colton, you sure are a good sport about all this," said Robert.

"I'll take that as your agreement to discuss business before dinner."

Robert laughed and smacked Colton on the shoulder. The wet sound made me shiver. "Sure. I guess you've earned it."

18

Frances

The savory smell of fried onions and peppers wafted into the bedroom. I hadn't realized I was hungry until my stomach rumbled in protest. Turning over my phone, I read the time: six o'clock. I quickly shot Marco a text, letting him know that everything was fine. Then I headed downstairs.

Marie was in the kitchen, stirring a large pot, steam rising from three other pans in front of her. "What are you cooking?" I asked, coming up beside her.

"Chili with some fried beans and vegetables."

"Smells delicious. Can I help with anything?"

"You can give Paul a hand with the fire," she flicked her head in the direction of the dining room. Paul threw some kindling in the fireplace and had just torn off a piece of the newspaper when I reached him.

"Your mom asked me to help you, but it looks like you have everything under control," I said, standing next to him.

He chuckled and crumpled up the paper in his fist before throwing it into the pit. "That's all right. I appreciate the company."

"Where's Colton and your dad?" I asked, stretching my neck to peek past the kitchen.

"They're in my father's study, talking business."

"Oh. Maybe I should go in there and see if Colton needs me to take notes or anything." I moved past Paul, but he put a hand on my shoulder to stop me.

"I don't think any note-taking will be necessary. I think Colton will be the one doing most of the talking. If I know my father, he's probably drilling him about everything but that property."

I pulled out one of the plush dining room chairs and sat down. "Do you think your father is going to sell him the land?"

Paul clicked his tongue. "You never know where you stand with my dad until he tells you. He has the best poker face."

"He's also got a good football tackle from what I've seen."

He barked out a laugh this time, and I couldn't help but smile. It was easy talking to him. He didn't make me feel uncomfortable or self-conscious. His demeanor put me at ease, as though we'd been friends for a long time.

Striking a match against the fireplace, Paul threw it into the kindling. He added a few logs and the fire roared to life. "You make that look easy," I said. "Do you build fires for a living?"

"I wish. No. I handle media and internal relations at Morgan and Son. I don't build fires, but I do help put them out."

"Any fires happening right now we should know about?"

When he turned to me, his eyes searched my face for a second before he said, "Nothing right now. But if you stick around I'll be happy to show you how it's done."

I gave him a weak smile. "I'm not interested in drama or fires. I prefer to stay away from the spotlight."

"Maybe. But my father recognized something in you, which means there's a spark there somewhere."

I was starting to feel it, too. The fire that had once burned inside me rekindled.

***

Colton and Robert joined us in the dining room shortly before dinner. I tried reading Colton's face, but he gave no indication that his private meeting went well. We sat next to each other at dinner, Paul and his mother across from us and Robert at the head of the table.

"Is everything all right?" I whispered when the family was distracted talking about the baby's christening.

"I'm not sure," said Colton, shortly after Marie wished us *bon appètit.*

"I just don't know how this will all work," he continued, rubbing the palm of his hand against his jeans. He looked up and his eyes held mine. Now, I wasn't sure if his words were about his meeting with Robert or us. The way his eyes warmed up my insides made my heart ache.

"I want it to work out," he said in a low voice. "But I just don't know."

"Frances," said Marie, "You haven't touched your dinner. Do you not like it?"

Taken aback by her interruption, I picked up my fork and took a bite. "Mmm, it's delicious," I said, even though I barely tasted a thing through the sour taste in my mouth from Colton's words.

Dinner dragged on and I was exhausted by the time Marie served her "famous" apple pie. Shortly afterward, I thanked them for their hospitality and said I would turn in early for the night.

"I'll walk you upstairs," said Colton, rising from his seat.

He followed me up the stairs, and my heart raced at the thought of him watching me. Despite everything that happened between us, I couldn't deny I still had feelings for him.

Colton walked me to my bedroom door and I turned to face him. He stared into my eyes again and I wanted to tell him everything at that moment. That I was sorry, that I still wanted him. When he pushed a strand of my hair back behind my eyes, I nearly did.

"Colton," I whispered, and reached for him. He caught my hand mid-air and closed his eyes. His brow furrowed and I saw him struggle but didn't know what he was thinking. When he opened his eyes, they seemed sad. He kissed my knuckles, then pushed off the door trim and left me standing there with nothing but the truth inside my heart—too afraid to open myself to someone. Too afraid to get hurt, again.

So, what did I want? Did I still want a relationship with Colton? Am I willing to fight for one?

I was still berating myself five hours later, lying in bed, completely awake at two in the morning. Throwing the comforter off of me, I grabbed my sweater and pulled it over my head. I'd changed into a pair of shorts and a t-shirt for bed, but a chill permeated the air now.

I considered walking over to Colton's room to see if he was awake, but knew it would look terrible if someone caught me in there at this hour. So, I tiptoed downstairs and walked to the kitchen looking for a small pot to boil water for tea. I didn't want to use a kettle and wake up the entire house. But when I reached the kitchen, my eyes caught a figure in the dining room. He sat facing the fireplace, his legs outstretched in front of him, balancing a half-empty glass on his thigh.

"Couldn't sleep either?" he asked in that familiar deep voice of his. It sounded rough right now, as though he hadn't spoken in months.

"No," I said, coming to stand beside him. Colton stared ahead at the dark and cold fireplace. White light from the moon shone on the left side of his face, illuminating his features enough for me to see the straight line of his lips and creased forehead. "What's wrong?" I asked.

"Just have a lot on my mind, that's all." He sipped his drink and brought it back down to his knee.

"How did the meeting go with Morgan this afternoon? We didn't get a chance to speak about it."

"All right, I guess. He asked a lot of questions but didn't give me many answers."

I nodded, figuring Morgan would have said something at dinner had they struck a deal. Knowing I had to say the next part didn't make getting the words out any easier. Wrapping my arms around my waist and clenching my sweater, I took a deep breath in.

"I'm glad I found you here," I said. "We need to talk."

He nodded but said nothing more.

"I tried earlier, but it didn't seem like you wanted to hear it. I want to apologize, Colton. I'm so sorry." The tears I'd held back for weeks finally fell, and despite my tears, I felt relief at finally purging my soul. "Do you think you could ever forgive me?"

"Frances, I forgave you the moment I realized why you had done it," he said, then dropped his head back against the plush chair and closed his eyes. "I just can't forgive myself for falling for it."

My heart clenched at the pain in his voice. I wanted to tell him not to use his past to ruin his present, but I would be the last person to suggest that to anyone else.

"You looked so upset when you left earlier. I thought you were still upset with me."

"I wasn't upset. Just confused. I'm not sure what's going on here between us, Frances."

"Me neither."

"I just know when you're near me, the smell of you, the sound of your voice, every movement of your body, calls to me." He reached for my hand and clasped our fingers together. "Right now, I just want to pull you into my arms and press my lips over every inch of your body."

I gulped. His words seared my heart with their intensity, and the heat from them spread everywhere.

"Are you saying you want to work through what happened?" I asked, hating the neediness in my voice.

"I don't know," he said, letting go and running his hand through his hair.

"What do you want, then?" I asked, angry at him now for giving me hope. I moved to stand in front of him. And waited.

Finally, he raised his eyes to look at me, and they held mine tighter than any embrace ever had. I couldn't move.

"You," he said. "I want you."

Relieved, I exhaled in one loud breath and whispered, "Then come get me."

He stared at me for only a second before, in one fluid motion, Colton placed his glass on the dining room table and pulled me into his arms. I took a breath, then his lips sealed mine and consumed the very air I breathed. Pressing myself against him, I couldn't get close enough. "I need you," I whispered next to his ear.

I felt goosebumps rise on the back of his neck, and then he bent down and scooped me up into his arms.

I held on tightly, wrapping my arms around his neck as he carried me up the steps and into my room. He laid me on the bed, but did not follow. I knew he did so to protect me. He knew I would tense up, and I loved him more for it. Standing above me next to the bed, he lifted his shirt, exposing the smooth ridges of his stomach. I reached for him and ran my fingers along his skin. Closing his eyes, he inhaled deeply, his nostrils flaring as I inched my way down.

"I want to take my time with you this time," he said, opening his eyes.

Ignoring him, I pulled my sweater over my head.

His eyes fell to my bare breasts and he groaned. "You aren't making this any easier on me, are you?"

I laughed and he simply shook his head. "Well, you're going to regret that."

I waited for his onslaught of kisses, but they didn't come. Instead, he dropped to his knees in front of me and pulled me to the edge of the bed. "Colton?" I asked, pulling myself up to stare at him.

"Shh. Lay back and relax."

How could I relax when he was about to do that? He pulled down my shorts and panties in one swift movement. *Impressive.*

I stared up at the ceiling, emotions spinning like a tornado inside my head. Did I want this? *Yes.* Was I sure? *No.* "It's all right, Colton. You don't have to do this," I said, wondering if he thought I'd expected this.

He rubbed his hands along my hips and his nose inched closed on my thigh. "I don't *have to*?" he asked.

I shook my head. "It's okay if you don't want to."

"*Sweetheart*," he purred. "I've wanted your taste on my tongue from the moment I saw you."

Then he swiped his tongue along my clit, and I shivered. All thoughts scattered from my mind, except for one. Please god, let him do that again. And he did. Over and over again until I moaned in pleasure.

The world faded around me to black. I couldn't see. I could only feel Colton's hands gripping my thighs and his breath on my sensitive flesh. A tingling sensation rushed to my core, building my body into a fever pitch. Hot pressure built inside me until I had to arch my back and clench the sheets to hold on and not buck him off of me. I didn't want to do that. I didn't want him to stop. Not now, not ever.

I moaned louder and Colton's hand shot up to cover my mouth as his tongue circled faster. I licked his fingers, but then pressed down on my lips when the pleasure became too much. He sucked harder on my clit until my tense body finally exploded in release. This time, I did buck up my hips, but Colton held them in place, licking me slowly until he lapped up every last shiver of my pleasure.

Spent, I dropped my hips onto the mattress and threw my arm over my eyes.

"Not yet, *baby*," he said, unzipping his pants and crawling on the bed beside me. He raised my other arm above my head and dropped his face between my breasts. Running his fingers down my arms, then gently across my nipples, a familiar tingling in my core started again. I squeezed my thighs together to relieve the pressure slowly building, but my body wanted more. It wanted all of him.

With both hands on his chest, I pushed Colton down onto the mattress and straddled him. He smiled but shook his head. "Not this time," he whispered.

"Yes, Colton," I said. "It's the only way that will work for me."

As much as I knew he wouldn't hurt me, I didn't want to risk my body's reaction and ruin this for us.

"Do you trust me, Frances?"

"You know I do, but this, this is different."

He rubbed his hands along my arms until he cupped my face. Pulling me down, he kissed my lips softly, gently. He kissed me until no other thought ran through my mind. Until I only saw Colton behind my closed eyes, only felt his tongue move down my neck. He laid me down beside him, his lips moving to my jaw as his hands guided me onto my side.

He caressed my breasts until my nipples hardened into sensitive peaks. Gently, he spooned beside me and nestled himself between my legs. Sweeping my hair off my neck, he ran his tongue just below my earlobe. The sensation raised tiny hairs all over my body.

Placing a hand on my inner thigh, he raised my leg high enough to adjust himself until he slid into me from behind. He wasn't deep inside, but the angle was so good. I hummed when he pressed his palm against my lower abdomen, massaging my g-spot. "Right there," I whispered.

Colton pushed in deeper, raising himself onto his elbow. My arms were free and he didn't hold me down, but he embraced me and loved me in this position. I never thought I could make love this way, and the revelation of his thoughtfulness brought tears to my eyes. "Colton," I whispered.

"I'm right here, *sweetheart*," he said. "Let go. I've got you." He rocked into me a little faster, pressing down a little harder, and I felt myself on the brink of climax again. He moved his hand further down and pressed down on my clit. My leg shook and my body trembled as I climaxed so hard I lost my breath.

The intimacy of the position and the consideration overwhelmed me and tears ran down my face. Colton quickened his pace until he gave one final, deep thrust and shouted his release into my neck. Falling back onto the mattress, he pulled me on top of him. As I laid my cheek on his chest, I prayed he didn't feel the wetness of my tears on his skin.

He ran his fingers through my hair and down my spine. Moving them up and down, and back again. The motion soothed me and allowed me a moment to catch my breath.

"There's nothing I want more than to spend the night with you, but I don't think Morgan would appreciate it." His voice sent shivers over my skin.

I nodded, lifting my head from his chest. He pulled me down and kissed my lips, slowly. "Maybe just a few more minutes," he groaned.

Smiling and replete, I snuggled beside him and closed my eyes.

19

Colton

A ray of light shone across her bare back, and I raised the sheet to cover her. I considered waking her, but I wanted a few more minutes to feel her soft curves against me. This was only the second time I'd slept with someone and spent the night. Sleeping with Frances in Miami was the first time. It was nothing to boast about. It was sad, really. However, I felt nothing but contentment right now. When I ran my fingers down her back, she murmured something against my chest, her breath caressing my skin.

"Frances," I whispered, but she didn't move. I smiled at the challenge. Moving my hand further down, I cupped her soft backside and lifted her on top of me. That was better. My body agreed.

"Colton," she whispered, but her eyes were still closed.

"I'm right here, beautiful," I said, running my hand through her hair.

"What time is—" she bolted straight up, the sheet falling at my feet. "Oh my god, we have to make breakfast. We lost the football game."

I didn't give a shit about football or breakfast at that moment when a naked Frances sat in front of me. Despite the panic on her face, I noticed her swollen lips from last night and I couldn't bring myself to feel guilty about it.

"Why are you smiling?" she asked.

"Because you're adorable when you panic."

She scurried off the bed, taking the sheet with her. "Where are my clothes?" She found them next to the door. I stretched out, putting my hands behind my head as I watched her dress.

"Aren't you going to get up?" she asked, annoyed.

"In a minute. Just enjoying the view."

She threw my shorts at me and growled. I grabbed them mid-air and pulled them on.

"I'll go downstairs and get started."

"I'll be down in a minute. Just need to take a quick shower."

Pointing a finger at me, she said, "You've got one minute, Colton."

"Yes, ma'am." I padded over to her and pulled her in for a kiss.

After she left, I waited another minute before opening the door again. Listening for any movement, hoping not to bump into Morgan, when I walked out into the hallway. Silence.

I stepped into the bathroom and turned on the water. Pressing both palms against the wall, I watched the rivulets fall from my skin. As I stood there, naked and alone, I realized for the first time that I didn't want to wash someone off of me. I didn't want to say goodbye and not see her again. Miami felt like a dream, but this was real.

By the time I entered the kitchen, everyone was already downstairs. Frances had pulled her hair up into a messy bun and threw a beige sweater on top of her t-shirt and shorts. She stood in front of the stove pouring batter into the pan.

"Do you know how to scramble eggs?" she asked when I placed my hand on her waist.

"Every bachelor does." I winked at her and grabbed a bowl next to the stove. She rolled her eyes at me, but a smile tugged at her lips. I loved making her smile.

We worked side by side at the stove while the Morgans set the table and poured the orange juice. My brothers and I shared dinners, but Luke did all the cooking. I never complained, but there was something to be said about whipping up a meal with someone. It brought two people together in ways that one person preparing alone couldn't do.

I saw when she hesitated about adding cinnamon to the pancakes and I whispered, "go for it." I loved the chuckle she gave me when she knew I'd read the indecision on her face. Or when she lowered the heat on my pan when I was busy grabbing the milk. I'd never thought domesticity would make me want a woman more. I thought it'd make me run. No, the lies had done that.

We all sat down at the kitchen table, and Marie kicked off the meal with her *bon appètit*. I scooped some eggs onto my plate, then passed them along to Robert.

"Crawford, I must say, I trust a man who can cook. Shows me he's patient," said Robert.

Patience wasn't my strong suit and I didn't want Robert to think I'd wait patiently for his signature. "If you can trust me enough to eat what I've cooked for you, you can trust me in business. Right, Morgan?" I brought a forkful of eggs to my mouth and waited for his response.

"Mmm," was all he said.

"The pancakes are delicious, Frances. Oh, I bet my homemade jam would be perfect on these. Would you like to try it?" Marie asked, already rising from her seat.

"Of course I would." Frances barely got the words out before Marie grabbed a jar of strawberry jam from inside one of the cabinets. There were at least twenty more stacked in there.

After trying the spread, Frances gave an approving hum. "You should consider selling these, Mrs. Morgan," she said.

"You really think so?"

Frances nodded, "Absolutely, I do. There are some farmer's markets I can suggest to you in town. My brother and grandmother go every weekend."

"Thank you, dear," said Marie, beaming at her. "You certainly knew what you were doing when you hired this one," said Marie, looking straight at me.

I glanced at Frances and she nearly choked on her pancakes, but I smiled. "I don't know if I knew exactly who I was hiring... but I think I'm finally starting to appreciate her." Frances's smile lit up the room, despite her trying to hide it with the back of her hand. I smiled openly at her.

Feeling like I could conquer the world after last night and this morning, I tried my luck with Robert. "If you have some time after breakfast, why don't we discuss a few things in your study, Morgan?" I asked.

He puckered his lips, and his white mustache twitched. "I have a better idea," he said. "Why don't I take you and Frances to see the escarpment? There's a wonderful looking-point we can walk to from here?"

The last thing I wanted was to go on another outing with Robert and his son. But if that's how Morgan wanted to play this out, so be it. "Sounds good," I said, and sipped my orange juice to hide my annoyance.

Frances placed her hand on my thigh, and the gesture calmed me down. Wrapping my hand over hers, I squeezed, hoping she understood my gratitude. Losing my cool with Morgan would not win me any points with him.

After breakfast, Mr. and Mrs. Morgan left to collect supplies for our day trip, and Frances excused herself to go upstairs. Watching her quit the room, I noticed Paul doing the same.

What's up with this guy? I hardly knew anything about him.

"What do you do for fun, Paul?" I asked, curious, but mainly wanting to redirect his eyes away from Frances.

"Huh?" he asked, directing his attention to me.

"I said, how do you unwind?"

"Oh. Well, I'm not usually wound up. So not much, I guess." He smiled and folded his hands in front of him. I gave him one of my best 'don't shit me' smiles, head tilt and all, and his grin faltered a bit.

"Really? Nothing ever gets you riled up?" I asked.

"I wouldn't say 'nothing', but it takes quite a lot."

"Well, it doesn't take much for me," I said. "I especially get riled up when someone tries to take something that's mine. Do you understand what I'm saying, Paul?"

"I don't think I do, Colton," he said, rising from the table. "All I see is you want to lay claim on something you haven't earned yet. Including my father's land."

I *wanted* to wipe that smug smile off his face, but I somehow kept my cool. "Making plans for the property and staking a claim is not the same thing. I have told no one that your father's property is mine, but I'd love to make it official this weekend."

"Perhaps, like winning a particular woman's heart, you should consider there's more competition out there than you think." He stood from the table and walked toward the stairs.

Sitting at the kitchen table, his words echoed repeatedly in my head.

More competition than you think.

I knew Paul had his eye on Frances, but who else was trying to purchase Morgan's property? Who else would want to build there? I had to find out and squash their plans before this competition was something I needed to worry about. Pulling out my cell phone, I dialed Ryan's number.

"Colton, what's up?"

"I need you to look into something for me," I said, looking around, but speaking in a low voice, just in case.

"What's that?"

"Find out if any other company has requested a land survey from the city of Morgan's property. We may have some competition."

"You got it," said Ryan, and hung up the phone.

Shoving my cell phone into my back pocket, I took the stairs to the second floor two at a time.

Morgan's property already had the mayor's approval for commercial development and it was close to a highway, so any commercial land developer would want it, perhaps even a residential one.

"Colton?" Frances called when I passed her bedroom door. Her hair was wet, but she was dressed in jeans and a blue sweater. "What's wrong?" she asked, pulling her hair back into a ponytail.

Scanning the hallway and finding it empty, I walked into her room and stood in front of the window. "Paul and I just had a little chat," I said, staring at the lake, trying to quiet my racing thoughts. "He insinuated that another company may have an interest in Morgan's property."

"What makes you say that?"

"He said there may be more competition out there than I had thought."

"Did he say which company?" she asked.

I shook my head. "No."

Frances put her hand on my back. "Any chance he's just trying to play games with your head?"

"Maybe," I said, and turned to face her. "I was trying to intimidate him. This could be his way of getting back at me."

"Why were you trying to intimidate him?" she asked.

"You know, you may be on to something, Frances," I said, snapping my finger. "I should call Ryan back and ask him to hire the same investigator he used for you to confirm if there's another company interested in Morgan's land." I pulled out my phone to call Ryan.

"*What*?" The word was barely a sound, but I heard it. I heard the shock behind it as well. Then it hit me—what I'd just blurted out.

"Frances, that came out wrong," I said, turning her to face me. Her eyes were unfocused as they bounced along my face.

"When?" she asked.

"When, what?"

She curled her fists. "When did you hire the investigator?"

"As soon as we got back from Miami."

She shook her head. "I don't understand. You hired an investigator after we'd been intimate together? You hired someone to look into my personal life and past?" she asked, her eyes finally holding onto mine.

I shook my head. "I didn't hire him. Ryan did."

Her eyes still held mine. "But you knew about it?"

"Yes."

She stepped back, out of my reach. "You knew your brother hired an investigator to look into things that were private to me and you were all right with that?"

"I was trying to prove to him that you had nothing to hide. But you were hiding something."

She paced the room. "I'd always thought Ava had come to you, that she had followed up on her resume. I'd never imagined this."

Water filled her eyes, but she kept the tears at bay. Knowing I was causing her such pain angered me. I didn't want to hurt her. Why was she taking this the wrong way?

"I don't know why you're upset with me. You were the one lying."

She grabbed her bag from under the bed and started packing her clothes in it.

"What are you doing?" I asked, panicked.

"I need to go home. I can't be here anymore."

"Fine. I'll just tell Morgan that we're leaving early."

"Not we, Colton, me. I don't want to drive over an hour in the car with you. I'm calling myself a cab or something."

"Don't be ridiculous. I'll drive you home."

"I don't want to be near you right now."

"I can take you back," another voice said from the hallway. Paul stood at France's door. "I'm heading into town myself. I can drive you home, Frances."

"That's not necessary," I said. "Frances, let's talk about this."

"Thank you, Paul." She grabbed her bag and pushed past me toward the door. Before disappearing down the hallway, she turned to me and said, "Goodbye, Colton."

"Frances, wait," I called after her. But she was already racing down the staircase.

I rushed back to my room to pack my things, hoping to catch her before she left.

The slamming of a car door drew me to the front window. Frances sat in the passenger seat while Paul spoke to his parents.

What the fuck just happened?

Frances

The drive back with Paul was quiet. He didn't speak much and I was grateful for it. When he pulled into my driveway, however, he broke his silence. "I like you, Frances," he said.

I smiled to soften the harshness of my words. "You just met me yesterday."

He grinned back. "I only needed a few minutes to know that I liked you." He shifted in his seat and raised my hand to intertwine with his. "And I'd like the opportunity to get to know you better."

His offer flattered me and I was tempted to try a date with him

—he was friendly—but I just couldn't say the words. "You seem like a nice guy," I began.

"Oh, god, don't say that." He laughed. "Don't say you just want to be friends."

I sighed but tried to smile again. "I won't say it then. But things are complicated for me right now and I don't want to add to it."

"I would be just another complication, then?"

I nodded.

"Okay, how about you give me your number and we stay in touch? No pressure, just want to say hello from time to time."

I was about to turn him down but reconsidered. Maybe I wasn't thinking properly at that moment and would regret closing the door to Paul later. "Sure," I said instead. I held out my hand and he rummaged in his jacket pocket and pulled out his phone so we could exchange numbers.

"There," I said, passing the phone back to him. He stared at it for a minute and then looked up through blonde eyelashes. "I'm glad you came this weekend. I hope we can do it again sometime."

"Thanks, Paul." I opened the car door but popped my head back in. "I'll see you around."

I watched him pull back onto the road and drive off.

When I opened the front door, a familiar scene greeted me. Sunday afternoons were my favorite. My entire family was home and after eating a large Sunday lunch, we usually watched movies or played cards. It appeared they had decided on the former.

"What are you guys watching?" I asked, placing my bag next to the stairs.

"Pride & Prejudice," mumbled Marco.

"The BBC version?" I asked.

"Of course," said my mother. "How was your work thing?"

"Fine," I said. "I'm heading upstairs for a bit."

"Are you hungry, *bella*?" my *Nonna* asked.

"No. I'm fine." I walked up the stairs and threw myself onto my bed. A few minutes later, a knock sounded at my open door.

"Can I come in?" Marco asked. I nodded but otherwise didn't move from my spot.

"That bad?" He pulled the chair from my tiny wooden desk and set it next to the bed.

Pushing my hair out of my face, I said, "What do you mean?"

"You told Mom you were fine, twice. That most definitely means that you're not."

I wanted to smile and cry at the same time. "How did you get to be so smart, huh?"

"I learned from you." He grinned his boyish grin.

Pushing myself off the bed, I sat cross-legged and faced my brother. "I quit my job at the store, and while Colton said he would pay me for this weekend, the way things ended, I don't know that he will."

"He will."

I shook my head. "How are you so sure?"

"He doesn't seem the type to talk shit. You know what I mean?"

I shrugged because I thought I knew Colton but wasn't so sure anymore.

"That wasn't Colton's car that dropped you off." It wasn't a question, and I started to resent that our family room window faced the driveway.

"No. That was Paul."

"Paul?"

"Paul Morgan. He's the prospective partner's son." Playing with a pulled thread on my bed cover, I added. "He asked for my number."

"Wow, wearing a new perfume or something?"

I chuckled. "Yeah, or something."

"Maybe it's the new confidence I've noticed in you. Guys notice that stuff, too."

Keeping my head down, I gathered my thoughts. "Been thinking." Unsure where I was going with this, but wanted to say it out loud to someone. "Maybe I should apply for another PA position."

Marco leaned back in the chair and crossed his arms. "I think that's a good idea."

"You do?"

"Yep. It's about time too."

"You sound like Erika," I groaned.

"Ah, another reason to like her."

I chuckled. "Marco, you don't have a prayer with her. You need to move on."

"She'll come around. You'll see."

"Come here." I opened my arms, and Marco wrapped himself around me. "I remember when I could touch my shoulders whenever we hugged. Time is moving so fast. I wish I could stop it."

"You don't have to stop time, Frannie. Just start living."

"Thanks, Marco."

He slowly raised himself from the chair and moved away from the bed. "Now, I better get downstairs before Mom complains that I've missed the best parts with Mr. Collins."

After Marco left, I pulled out my laptop and worked on my resume. I uploaded it onto a couple of recruiting sites and saved a few positions I thought I'd be qualified for to look at later. Although I told myself I'd made progress, my body disagreed. My heart raced and a cold sweat ran down my back. I felt it every time I did something that scared me.

Enough, Frances. This ends now. I cleared the search bar and typed in mental health help. I narrowed down the search to local centers and wrote down on a sticky note the number of a clinic near me.

I needed to talk to someone about my fears. I couldn't deal with them alone anymore and I was tired of letting them run my life.

I needed help.

As I lay down on my bed, tears fell down my face. I let them run down my cheeks and trickle down to my jaw. They pooled behind my ears and I still didn't wipe them. Thoughts rioted in my head, shouting at me, screaming for attention.

What if one of those companies calls me back? What if no one did? Then louder. *Why did Colton lie to me? Why didn't I tell him the truth sooner?*

Whispering behind all the shouting was another voice. *You can't do this, Frances. Who do you think you are?* But that was Chris's voice. And I was done listening to him.

20

Frances

"Francesca, there's a letter here for you!" my grandmother shouted from the kitchen. When I reached the table, she placed the letter and a plate filled with pancakes in front of me.

"Sit. Eat." She pointed to the chair. I hadn't come down for breakfast in two days, claiming to be sick. I couldn't face my family having lost two jobs.

"Thanks, *Nonna*." I opened the envelope and pulled out a piece of paper along with a check totaling two weeks' pay for the PA position.

"Told you he'd come through," said Marco, looking over my shoulder. I crushed the letter against my chest and left the table to read it privately. I should've been happy when I realized it was a letter of reference for Frances Netto, but my heart had hoped it was something else from Colton. Not exactly sure what, but not this.

Dropping the letter on the front console, I grabbed my jacket and purse from the closet. "I'm going out," I called back before walking out the front door.

A cold breeze slashed through my hair and across my face as I struggled to tie it back. After zipping my jacket, I stuffed my hands in my pockets and walked toward the major intersection. We didn't live far from the main road; it only took me about ten minutes to reach it.

When trepidation scratched at my throat, I breathed deeply, pushing it down my chest.

You have to do this, Frances.

Passing the familiar pawnshops, fruit stalls, and discount stores, I didn't stop until I reached the medical building I'd found online the other night. Inside, I read the names of the services provided in the building. Noting the floor and room number of the mental health office, I took the stairs to the second floor. My hands shook and my teeth chattered, but it wasn't from the cold.

A woman sat at the front desk and looked up when I walked in. "Please take a number at the door." Looking around the room, I was the only one there. Despite wanting to say so, I grabbed a ticket and sat down.

"Number thirteen?" called the woman. I handed her my ticket. Finally, looking up, she asked, "Name?"

"Frances Netto."

"Reason for your visit?"

"I'd like to speak to someone."

"About?"

My life. But I didn't say that. "Um. Is there a therapist here or something?" I handed her my insurance card.

"Yes. I can book you in with Dr. Lee next month."

"Next month?"

"Yes. But if you need to talk sooner, Dr. Lee holds free walk-in group sessions each Tuesday night. She's holding one tonight if you wish to attend."

I nodded. "I'll still take that appointment, though."

"I already have you booked." She smiled and handed me back my card. Thankfully, my dad's union job had great benefits. I could hear my mom's voice now, begging me to apply for a position at his factory: *What more could you ask for, Frannie?* A lot more, Mom, I thought. I just never did.

Walking back home, I stopped at one of the fruit stalls to buy a pineapple. Marco liked adding them to his fresh smoothies. I was nearly home when my phone beeped in my back pocket. Hugging the pineapple awkwardly against my chest, I checked my message. It was an email from one of the recruiting agencies.

'Dear Ms. Netto,' the email read. 'We would like to arrange an interview with you at our office tomorrow at 4 p.m. Would you be available?'

Scanning the rest of the email, I realized the job interview was for Sterling Realty. They were the second-largest land developers in the city. Second to Crawford Corp. I'd be working for one of Colton's competitors. I hesitated for only a moment before I typed my reply.

'Thank you for considering me for the position. The date and time work for me. I look forward to chatting with you.' I hit send and stuffed my phone back into my pocket. I wasn't an employee of Crawford Corporation any more. I wasn't Colton's girlfriend, either. I had no reason to feel guilty about this. None.

So why did I feel like throwing up?

Nerves. I was just nervous. No one had interviewed me in nearly six years, not since Clive hired me for the mailroom right out of college. I needed practice, that was all.

I dropped the pineapple on the counter and texted Erika when I got home.

Me: Can you come over after work?

Erika: Sure. What's going on?

Me: I have a job interview tomorrow. A big one and I'd like you to help me practice.

Erika: Yay! I'm so proud of you. Of course, I'll be there. See you at 6!

"Everything okay, Francesca?" my *Nonna* asked, coming from the family room. *Wheel of Fortune* played in the background.

I smiled. "Yes, *Nonna*. At least it's going to be."

She came up to me and patted my cheek. "You're a smart girl, Francesca. *Nonna* loves you very much."

She had said this to me before, but this time I fought back tears. For the first time in a long time, I believed her. "Thank you, *Nonna*." My voice cracked and I hugged her before she could see the emotion in my eyes.

"Don't cry," she said, rubbing my back. "Everything will be okay."

I nodded and held her tighter. She was shorter than my five-foot-four stature, barely reaching five feet, but she was the strongest person I knew.

Pulling away from her, I wiped the tears that had escaped. "Oh, *Nonna*. Can you set an extra plate for dinner? Erika will be joining us."

"That's good," she said with a smile. "Marco will be very happy."

"Don't encourage him." I laughed and hurried upstairs.

A few hours later, having finished dinner, Erika sprawled herself on my bed as I tried on outfits for tomorrow. "Not that one," she said. "It makes you look old."

"This is the third one I've tried on," I complained. "I don't have any designer clothes in here to work with."

"You don't need designer clothes to look fashionable, trust me." She pushed herself up from the bed and stood in front of my closet with both hands on her hips. She pulled out a black blouse, a black pencil skirt, and a bright pink sweater. "Try these on."

After buttoning the sweater, I checked myself in the mirror. "Not bad," I said. "This could work."

Erika removed her black feathered headband and placed it on my head. "Now it's perfect." Staring back at me in the mirror, she smiled. "You got this, Frannie."

I nodded and pulled my shoulders back to stand up straighter. "I got this."

The next day, I asked Marco to drive me to the interview. It had snowed last night and I didn't want to bring an extra pair of shoes on the bus. However, when I sat in the car, my nerves got the best of me and I panicked.

What if I don't get the job? What if I do?

"Relax," Marco said when he spotted my knee bouncing in the passenger seat. "You're going to knock their socks off."

I looked out the window as we approached a large white building with a blue roof. "This is it." My stomach clenched and I bit my lip to hold in a groan. "Maybe it's not too late to cancel," I said.

"You rehearsed with Erika last night. I heard you. You were great. You've got nothing to worry about," he said. "Even if you don't get this job, I'm proud of you. I know this is a big step for you."

I turned to my little brother and smiled. "Thank you," I said and patted his cheek. "You're turning into *Nonna*, you know that?"

"Get out of my car before I take back what I said."

I laughed and grabbed my portfolio before I closed the car door. With a honk, he pulled out onto the street. The building was smaller than Crawford Corp, with fewer windows, too, but I felt more intimidated than when I applied for a job there. Walking up to the front doors, I inhaled deeply.

"Here goes nothing," I whispered, and stepped through the automated glass doors.

"I'm here to see Ms. Mahmoud. My name's Frances Netto," I told security at the front desk. After a brief phone conversation, he directed me to the fifth floor.

There was no reception desk when I stepped off the elevator, but a woman in a short bob waved me over from behind her glass-enclosed office. She sat with her arms crossed at her desk while she listened to a man on the other end. "I don't care what you have to do, Gerald, just get it done." She hit a button on the phone and rolled up the sleeves of her blazer. Leaning forward, she extended her hand toward me. "Frances? I'm Mariam Mahmoud, CEO of Sterling Realty."

I gave her my firmest handshake and sat down in the white linen chair across from her desk. "Thank you for coming on short notice," she said, her eyes trained on mine.

I nodded. "I'm glad I could make it work."

She quickly scanned a piece of paper on her desk. I assumed it was my resume. Then, she returned her attention to me. "To be honest, this resume is decent, but what caught my attention was the note at the bottom stating a reference letter from Colton Crawford, CEO of Crawford Corp. Do you have that letter with you today?"

"I do." I pulled the letter from my portfolio and placed it on her desk.

She yanked a pair of glasses out from her blazer and examined the paper. "Mmm. How long did you work there?"

I cleared my throat. "Six years in the mailroom. Then two weeks as Mr. Crawford's personal assistant."

She pursed her lips. "Two weeks, huh?"

I nodded and was about to thank her for her time when a tiny voice inside my head told me to fight.

"I know it wasn't a very long time, but I created a more efficient filing system for Mr. Crawford, researched new properties of interest for him, and worked on an upcoming development project. I learned a lot in the short amount of time I was there."

"Upcoming development project, did you say?" She tapped her bottom lip. "Does that project have anything to do with Robert Morgan's land?"

I kept my face serene. "I'm not at liberty to say, Ms. Mahmoud."

She pursed her lips. "I appreciate your discretion. It's something we'd expect from one of our employees as well." She tapped on the desk. "We need someone to start soon. My last assistant eloped and won't be returning."

"I can start tomorrow."

"Great." She stood from her desk again with her hand toward me. "Welcome to Sterling Realty."

***

Dr. Lee sat in a black ergonomic office chair, surrounded by wooden bookshelves, while I sat in a cream-colored armchair in front of her desk. It was plush and comfortable. This was my third session with Dr. Lee. I'd told her everything I'd ever wanted to say and things I'd never admitted even to myself, all in the first hour of meeting her. It was like verbal diarrhea once I started talking. She mostly listened and sometimes gave a task to complete before the next session.

"I think we're making great progress, Frances," she said, staring back at me through her black-rimmed glasses.

"Do you really think so?" I asked, folding my arms and sinking further into the chair.

"I do. You need to give yourself credit and be proud of what you've accomplished in such a short time."

Thinking back to when I stood inside the mailroom less than three months ago, watching the suits pass me by, and now, being one of them at Sterling Realty, I realized Dr. Lee was right.

"This week I want you to focus on building your social network." She scribbled on a notepad while she spoke. "I know it's not easy for you to make new friends, but how about you ask Erika for a girls' night out?"

"I can do that."

"Good. Maintaining a social network is important for you right now. I don't want you isolating yourself."

"I'll ask Erika. I promise." Checking my watch, I jolted up from the chair. "I've got to go."

"We still have a few more minutes."

"I was late for work last time. Although Mariam is more forgiving than Colton, I don't want to take advantage."

"We'll work on the people-pleasing next time," said Dr. Lee, scribbling on her notepad.

I chuckled. "Deal."

I rushed out of the medical building and chased after the bus before it reached its next stop. "Thanks, Donnie," I said to the driver.

"I don't know how you run in those heels," he said, shaking his head and using his whole body on the steering wheel to turn the bus back onto the street.

I made it to work on time, even though Mariam was already in her office. "Morning," I said before turning on my laptop.

"Good morning, Frances," she called, without taking her eyes off of her screen.

I put my head down and worked for the next three hours without saying a word. It wasn't until nearly noon that my stomach growled and I decided to break for lunch. Checking Mariam's afternoon schedule for anything urgent before I took my break, I noticed she'd booked a new meeting. The appointment was with "RM".

I knocked on her office door while she typed. "Come in," she called.

"Mariam, I'm checking if you need anything for your three o'clock meeting. I noticed you just added it to your schedule."

"Yes." She looked up and her blue light glasses slid to the edge of her nose. "Can you bring me the land registry for this address?" She wrote it down on a piece of paper.

"Not a problem." I picked up the note and brought it back to my desk.

Typing the address into my laptop, my heart sank when I saw the name of the property owner: Robert Morgan. Was Sterling the competition Paul had warned Colton about?

I printed out the land registry information and brought it to Mariam.

"Is your three o'clock meeting with Mr. Morgan?" My voice sounded hesitant, even to my ears.

"It is," she said

"Do you need me to set up the boardroom for you?"

"No, we're meeting at his office."

Mariam hadn't told me about this appointment, nor did she ask me to help her with a presentation. I wondered if this was the first meeting or the final one. She had kept me out of the loop, which only made me wonder why she had hidden it from me in the first place.

"Do you require me at this meeting?"

Mariam looked up and removed her glasses. "I know you've already met Morgan when you were working for Crawford Corp. I don't want any conflict-of-interest concerns, so I think it's best if I handle this one on my own. After we purchase the property, we can discuss how to proceed." Putting her glasses back on, she turned toward her laptop.

After? She sounded pretty confident in Morgan selling her the property. This would devastate Colton.

It's not your problem, Frances. Stay out of it.

I skipped lunch, having lost my appetite, and took a walk to clear my head. It didn't work. When I returned to my desk, I forced Colton out of my thoughts and focused on work instead.

Except I knew too much. I knew how much this property meant to him. I knew how hard he'd worked on his presentation, on the plans he had for Morgan's property and the land around it.

An idea popped into my head, but I quickly dismissed it. It wouldn't be ethical, *would it*? We were friends, though. He did say I could call him anytime, and Dr. Lee suggested I get out more. It would just be two friends having a drink. If business came up, well, that happened between friends sometimes, *didn't it*?

I found his number in my contacts and sent him a text.

Me: Hey Paul, it's Frances. How are you?

I didn't expect a reply right away, but I hoped for one. When the three dots appeared on my phone, my heart cheered. I sat clutching my phone, waiting...

Paul: Hello, Frances. It's great to hear from you. I'm good. How's everything with you?

Me: I was hoping we could grab a drink sometime, maybe catch up?

Paul: Would love to. Are you free this Friday? I can pick you up at six for dinner.

Did I want to have dinner with Paul? It would be easier to talk with him at a restaurant instead of a bar.

Me: This Friday works. Looking forward to it.

Paul: Me too.

That night, I called Erika and told her everything.

"What are you going to do, Frances?"

"I'm not sure. Find out if Robert Morgan is going to sell the property to Sterling."

"And if that's what they're planning? You can't stop them. I don't know what that's called, but you don't work for Crawford anymore, you work for Sterling. You got to decide, where do your loyalties lie?"

I wasn't sure yet, but I would find out tomorrow night.

21

Frances

Wall sconces and candles lit the restaurant. A man played the piano at the back while the aroma of food sizzling on a grill greeted us when we walked in.

"Bonjour, Madame. Bonjour, Monsignor Morgan," said the host when we approached the podium.

After looking around the room, Paul addressed the host. "Bonjour, Pierre. We have a reservation for seven this evening."

"*Bien sûr.*" The man checked the large book in front of him and scratched a pencil across the page.

"Follow me. We set a table near the back, as you requested."

Patrons filled every seat inside the restaurant, leaving only one empty table left after we claimed ours.

"May I take your coat, Madame?" the host asked me.

"I think I'll keep it a little while longer. I'm still a bit chilled."

I decided on the black shift dress I'd worn on my first day as Colton's PA. I should have brought my sweater, though.

"Have you ever been to Chez Jacques?" asked Paul, opening the menu in front of him.

"Never," I admitted, following suit. "Oh. Everything's in French. How wonderful." I groaned inwardly.

Paul chuckled. "I felt the same way the first time I ate here, too. Shall I order for both of us?"

"I'll just have the chicken," I said, and closed the menu.

A server appeared shortly afterward, a bottle in hand. "I've brought you your usual, Monsignor Morgan. Shall I pour?"

"Do you like red wine, Frances?"

"I do."

He waved the server forward to pour and swished the wine in his glass before taking a sip. "Lovely. You may proceed," he said.

As I watched the waiter pour my drink, Paul cleared his throat. "So, tell me, why did you text me the other day? I admit, I was surprised to hear from you, but flattered nonetheless."

"We're just going to get right to it?" I asked and took a large sip of the wine.

"I didn't think this would be the difficult part," he said, tilting his head. He had gelled back his blonde hair tonight and he wore a jacket with his dress shirt but no tie. He looked good. But I wasn't attracted to Paul.

"I wanted to speak to you, privately," I explained.

"I like where this is going." He smiled and raised his glass. "To new beginnings."

"Ah, that's sort of what I wanted to talk to you about." I picked up my glass and clinked it with his. "I was going to wait until dessert, but perhaps it's best if we have this discussion first."

"This sounds serious," he said, but softened his remark with a smirk.

After inhaling a deep breath, I blurted out, "Has your father decided to sell his property?"

Paul folded the black table napkin across his lap. "He is pretty close to making a decision, I'd say."

I pursed my lips. *Ask him! Don't overthink it—just do it!* "Does he plan to sell it to Sterling Realty or Crawford Corporation?"

Paul placed his elbows on the table and interlaced his fingers. "I understand you work for Sterling now, is that right?"

"It is."

"Are you here on business then, to pitch your new company to me?"

I shook my head. "No. The opposite, actually."

He raised his eyebrows at my admission. "I'm intrigued. What do you mean by that?"

I leaned forward, jamming my forearms onto the table. "Colton can be a real jerk to work with—I know this better than anyone. But he has great plans for that property. He has thought of every circumstance and provision and has figured out a way to make it work for the community for generations to come. He wants this to be a legacy of sorts. Colton plans to turn your land into something even your grandchildren will be proud of."

Paul inhaled a deep breath and leaned back in his chair. "Are you and Colton together? Romantically?"

I narrowed my eyes. "I wouldn't be here if we were."

"So, you are making this plea for what gain?"

"There's no gain for me. I just know what this means to him and I think it's a great plan. I just didn't want what happened at your cabin to influence any decision on your family's part."

"Well, I can't say that it won't. My father takes everything personally. More than I think he should." He folded his arms and held my gaze. "Why didn't you speak directly to my father about this?"

"Because he reminds me of my own dad. Stubborn." I shook my head. "He'd probably go with Sterling just to prove that he could."

Staring at me with a small smile on his lips, he asked, "You don't see me the same way?"

I shook my head. "I don't. I think you're more rational than emotional. I know I don't know you very well, but I think I'm a good judge of character."

He picked up his menu and raised his gaze above the leather binding. "Let's order, and perhaps I'll consider taking a closer look at Crawford's proposal when I'm back in the office." He smiled and I couldn't help smiling back.

"Thank you," I whispered, and opened the menu again.

Before I could read the first choice of appetizer, my body shivered and my eyes jumped toward the front doors. Still wearing his coat, Colton stood only ten feet away from me. His brother, Ryan, followed closely behind him. My heart stopped and sped up again. I wanted to run to him, but I gripped my chair instead, holding myself in place. My eyes, however, pleaded with him. I wanted him to know how much I missed him. Reading the look on his face, he didn't feel the same.

He stared at me, but betrayal burned in his eyes. When he fired a menacing stare at Paul, I realized what this must look like to him. Oh, he couldn't be further from the truth. Colton took a step toward us, but Ryan held him back.

His brother led him to the last empty table and pushed him into a chair. Colton's eyes never left mine. They held me captive. I blinked, wishing he'd release me from their hold, and the chaotic emotions raging through my body. But it didn't work.

"Excuse me," I said, and dropped my napkin onto the table. I pushed my chair back and rushed to the washroom. Reaching the end of the narrow hallway, the server directed me down a flight of stairs toward the basement. Footsteps followed me halfway down.

It's just another patron, Frances. You have nothing to be afraid of.

But before I could push against the bathroom door, two hands grabbed my shoulders and turned me around.

"What are you doing here with him?" Colton growled.

Despite the anger on his face, I didn't panic. I stood my ground and counted to five, waiting for my frantic heart to slow. Dr. Lee's voice rang in my ears, *Face your fears.*

"Frances?" Colton's voice was softer now. He ran a hand through his hair. "I'm sorry. I must have scared you. I'm just..."

He turned to face the wall and slammed his fist against it.

"Are you two seeing each other?" he asked, still facing the concrete.

"No," I said. The tendons spasming on his forearm caught my attention.

Turning to face me again, he asked, "Then why are you here?"

I sucked in my lips, not wanting to tell him I came to plead his case. I didn't know how he'd react to me interfering with his business.

"Are you trying to make me jealous? Wasn't it enough that you took a job to work for the competition?"

How did he know where I worked?

"Are you following me?" I asked.

His left eye twitched. "No. But as I mentioned, Ryan was looking into the matter and informed me of the company's latest acquisition —you. Is that why you're here with Paul?"

"No. Of course not." I couldn't breathe being this close to him, but I had to get the words out.

"I didn't know Mariam was speaking to Morgan until after I started. I didn't know she was after the same property as you. You have to believe me, Colton."

He stared at me and narrowed his eyes. I wanted to shout that I came here tonight for him, to convince Paul to speak to his father on Colton's behalf, but I didn't think he'd believe me, not with that skeptical look in his eyes. So, I went with another truth.

"I came here with Paul tonight because we needed to talk and also because my therapist said I should get out more."

His jaw relaxed, and his eyes widened, softening his features. "You're talking to a therapist?"

I nodded.

"That's good," he whispered, raising his hand toward my face, then shoving it back into his pocket. "I'm glad."

I closed my eyes, not wanting to analyze the compassionate look on his face any longer. When I opened them, I felt tired. Tired of not knowing where he stood. Was he still angry? *Was I?*

"What do you want, Colton?" I asked. "Why did you follow me down here?"

He opened his mouth to speak but ran his hand over his lips before whispering, "I don't know anymore."

I nodded. "Then let me pass."

He stepped back, but before I could turn around, he asked, "Why haven't you called me?"

"What?" I asked, incredulously.

He put a hand on his hip. "I was sure you'd call, want to talk about it, but you didn't."

I collected my thoughts. "I was angry with you. You didn't call me either when you were angry with me."

Breathe, Frances.

"No. I just came to your house to find you."

"That was different. That was because you needed me for work," I spoke calmly, but my heart hammered against my chest.

He stared at me, and his nostrils flared. "This is killing me. I don't understand what's going on. Makes me want to punch a hole right through this wall. But I feel like I'm the only one going crazy here." Running a hand through his hair again, he added, "Do you even think about us, about what happened?"

"Of course, I do."

"Then scream at me. Yell at me. Call me a bastard. Say anything because I can't take this silent treatment anymore." Finally, he allowed his hand close to my face, his fingers caressing my cheek. "I..." He swallowed. "I care about you, Frances."

My heart wanted to give in, but my pride wouldn't let it go. "People who care about each other don't hire private investigators."

"I didn't think he would find anything. I didn't think I would have to ask you if you were lying to me. Why didn't you tell me the truth? I would have understood had you come to me first."

"I was going to tell you that day, but you didn't have time for me. You were too busy with work. And then you didn't even give me a chance to explain before you fired me."

"Fine. We both lied to each other and should have been honest. Let's just move on."

"You don't get it, do you?"

"No, I don't."

"I lied, yes. But that was to my boss. When I fell in love, I knew I had to come clean to you. But you, you knew you were lying behind my back and did it, anyway."

"You know, I'm getting the feeling that you want to stay angry with me. I'm just fooling myself that you want more."

"I want..." I looked down.

"What do you want, Frances?"

I wanted to not be afraid of losing myself again. There, I admitted the crux of the problem to myself. I was afraid that if I got into a relationship again, I would lose all the independence that I'd gained. I felt it with Colton. I would do anything for him—I would give him all of myself.

I couldn't go through that again. Not when I'd come this far.

"I just can't," I said, and pushed past him and ran straight into the bathroom.

Pressing my back against the tiled wall, a sob squeezed through my throat. Tears streamed down my face and I didn't bother wiping them away. My heart broke. But it wasn't Colton who caused this ache. I did. It was my choice to keep pushing him away and I had to live with my decision.

A long while later, someone tapped on the door. "Frances, are you all right?" It was Paul. "Colton left. You don't have to worry about him."

Walking up to the sink, I cleaned up my makeup and stared in the mirror. I didn't have to worry about Colton anymore.

He was gone.

It was poetic justice that words meant to comfort me just tore my heart in half.

Colton

I stared at the bathroom door that separated me from Frances. I willed her to come out.

I wanted to tear the door down and go after her. Instead, I grabbed the casing on either side of the door and dropped my head. Squeezing the wood between my fingers, I was surprised it didn't crack.

Why won't she fight for us? Did I imagine her feelings for me?

I'd recognized the fear in her eyes when I'd shouted at her and knew I needed to back off, to give her some space. So, I pushed off the door and walked back upstairs.

"Let's go," I said to Ryan, walking past our table. I didn't even bother looking at the other guy. He was insignificant.

I'd driven to the restaurant and parked less than a block away. But I threw my keys at Ryan. "You drive," I barked.

Catching the keys in mid-air, he said, "I guess things didn't go well downstairs."

"No. They did not."

I dropped into the passenger seat and stared out the window.

"What happened back there?" asked Ryan once he started the car.

I sank further into the passenger seat and crossed my arms. I thought that would signal my disinterest in discussing the matter with my brother, but he didn't take the hint.

"Colton?" He turned to look at me. He wouldn't let it go.

"Nothing."

"Didn't look like nothing. What did she say?"

"She said she can't get past what happened," I muttered, rubbing my bottom lip with my finger.

"She said that?"

"Not in those words exactly, no," I mumbled. "But it's what she meant."

"You know, for a man that's dated a lot, you understand shit about women."

"Fuck off, Ryan."

He laughed, but I didn't find the conversation amusing.

A few minutes later, he asked, "Can you get past it? Can you forgive her?"

"Of course I can. I already forgave her. She's the one who's still mad at me."

"I don't think you were ever mad at Frances for lying to you. I think you were mad that someone you cared about fooled you again."

I hated him. I hated that he'd said it aloud to me. Hated it because it was the truth I'd realized long ago but thought I could hide it from my brothers.

"Yeah. I get it. I screwed up before. Lost it all and now I can't be trusted to figure things out on my own."

"Colton, it doesn't matter how many times we tell you it wasn't your fault and that we forgive you. Brother, it won't matter until you forgive yourself."

"I don't get you, Ryan. It's why you did it. It's why you hired the investigator. You're the one who wanted to prove she was lying. Now you want me to get her back?"

"Yeah. Your worst fear just came true. So, what are you going to do about it? Face it or run from it?"

I ground my back teeth until my jaw hurt.

He pounded on the steering wheel with the palm of his hand. "Get your head out of your ass and fight for what you want."

"I am fighting!" I shouted. "She's the one that doesn't want to fight for us."

"Just because she's not shouting doesn't mean she isn't fighting."

Damn it! Was she fighting? Was there still a chance for us?

22

Frances

Sterling Realty wasn't a large office, but the personalities of its sales team made up for its size. A few of the top-selling agents exchanged back slaps and handshakes. Their latest celebration was taking over the office. I stayed in my seat despite my colleagues inviting me for a glass of champagne. I wasn't in the celebratory mood.

I walked over to the printer to pick up the copies of the presentation I'd made for Mariam's afternoon meeting. We had a busy schedule today and I looked forward to losing myself in my work.

I hadn't called Colton, even though I held the phone in my hands every night, willing myself to do so. What would I even say—I'm sorry for lying? I wasn't. I forgive you for treating me like some cheating spouse. Of course not; I was obviously still sour about it. I needed more time.

My desk vibrated and a message pinged on my phone. My heart jumped. Slowly, I picked up my cell phone and saw Marco's name on the screen. I wasn't sure if I was relieved or disappointed. Maybe both.

Marco: Clear your schedule tonight. We're all going to Zia Lisa's house for dinner.

My aunt Lisa was my mother's sister. We lived only a few blocks away from her family and grew up alongside her kids. We often had dinner at each other's homes, but it had been a few months since we'd gotten together.

Me: Mom and dad coming too?

Marco: Yup. We'll probably start a card game.

I wasn't in the mood to sit across from my uncle Tony asking me why I didn't have a boyfriend, then listen to him offer me his reasons why. Besides, having the house to myself sounded too good to be true.

Me: Thanks, but tell Zia that I can't make it. Tell her I'll be working late.

Work was a great excuse for my family. No one questioned or criticized it. Work came first. If you had to work, then you had to work.

Marco: You don't really, do you? ☹

Why did Marco have to know me so well?

Me: Have fun!

"Frances," Mariam called from her office. I threw my phone in my bag and carried the printouts to her desk.

"These are for our meetings this afternoon," I said, handing them to her.

"Thank you. But that's not why I called you in here."

I bit the inside of my cheek, wondering if she would ask me about my sour mood. But she didn't. Instead, she asked, "Do you know Morgan's PA?"

"Morgan's PA?" *Why would she want to know that?*

"I'd said I wouldn't involve you, but Robert Morgan has stopped returning my calls and my emails have gone unread. Just wondering if he's purposely ignoring me or if something happened to him."

I wondered about that myself. "Yes. I've spoken to his PA before. I'll give her a call this afternoon."

"Thanks. Oh, and Frances. Just wanted to say, I think you're doing a great job. I'm happy to have you onboard."

I forced my lips into a smile, even though I felt guilty about last night's conversation with Paul. Was Robert ignoring her? Would the PA even know that? Probably. Personal assistants knew everything about their bosses, even if their bosses weren't aware that they knew.

Although I told Mariam I would call Diane this afternoon, I called her as soon as I got to my desk. I wanted to get the phone call with Colton's ex over with as soon as possible.

"Robert Morgan's office. How can I help you?" *That wasn't Diane's voice.*

I wondered if she still worked there.

"Is Diane there?" I asked.

"She's off this week. This is Jill. What can I do for you?"

"Hey, Jill. This is Frances Netto calling from Mariam Mahmoud's office at Sterling Realty."

"Great. How can I help you?" Jill sounded chipper, if a bit rushed. So, I cut the formalities and got right to it.

"Listen, is Robert around? Mariam's been trying to get a hold of him, but he hasn't responded."

"He's been at his cabin most of the month and hasn't taken any new business meetings. Wait, hold on." Jill clicked away at her keyboard. "Yes. He has a meeting this afternoon with Colton Crawford. Did you want me to book something tomorrow for Mariam?"

"That would be great."

A few more clicks. "Done. She's in at four."

"Thanks, Jill. I really appreciate it." I rushed off the phone and knocked on Mariam's open door.

When she looked up from her computer, I said, "I got you a meeting with Morgan tomorrow at four o'clock."

"Great work," she said, a broad smile spreading across her face.

"Let's work on a new proposal after today's meetings. You don't mind staying late, do you?"

"Not at all," I said, relieved that my earlier lie to Marco turned out to be the truth.

I worked all afternoon, running between board meetings and working on Mariam's new proposal for Morgan. I prepared her slides and read through the presentation. It wasn't as good as Colton's, but that didn't mean Morgan wouldn't go for it. Perhaps he would prefer Sterling's simpler subdivision plan instead of the high-end shopping destination Colton had proposed. Finally, at six o'clock, I submitted the presentation to Mariam, and she approved it.

"Thanks for your help today," she said as I wished her a good night.

"My pleasure." I walked out, feeling a little better than I did when the day started.

I was good at my job. I had made headway in my life with Dr. Lee's advice and I was finally feeling like the person I was meant to be. If only I could get my love life together. Maybe I'd call Colton tonight. Ask him how his meeting went? No, I needed to be honest with him. More direct. I pulled out my phone before I lost my nerve.

Me: Hey, about last night... I'm hoping we can finish that conversation. Maybe we can talk later?

By the time the bus stopped in front of the pawnshop at the corner of my street, Colton still had not responded to my text. Staring at the phone wouldn't make him text me any faster, so I shoved the phone in my purse and vowed not to check it until later. It didn't stop my heart from wanting him to respond or my mind from replaying our words from last night. I wished I could have that night back. I wished I could have told him that despite everything, I still loved him.

Perhaps it was my melancholy, but when I opened my front door,

I missed my *Nonna* calling out to me, asking how my day went. Maybe it wasn't too late to join my family.

I climbed the steps to my bedroom, deciding I would make myself a sandwich, then go to *Zia's* house to distract me from staring at my phone the whole night. That sounded like a good plan. But first I had to change. I couldn't spend another minute in this skirt and blouse.

Opening one of my drawers to grab a pair of tights, I froze. I thought I'd heard a noise.

Creak.

What was that?

I peeked outside my window and spotted Chris's truck in my driveway. Panic set in and I couldn't breathe.

Don't open the door. He'll go away.

I ran to my purse and pulled out my phone, preparing to dial.

Creak.

Footsteps on the staircase, I was sure of it. Then the thump of boots hitting our parquet floor upstairs. I closed my eyes, imagining myself seven years ago and spiraling back to that dark place.

My bedroom door opened and the face of my nightmares stood before me again.

"Frannie," he said. His voice was soft, like a serpent's tongue.

"How did you get inside?" My voice sounded distant, as though it traveled through a tunnel first.

My mind retreated as I found myself alone with Chris in my bedroom. My eyes moved toward the closet and I shuddered.

"Your family still hides the key in a hole between the bricks." He took a step closer to me and while I physically didn't move, every muscle in my body tensed.

I clenched my fists at my sides and steadied my voice. "I want you to leave, Chris. Now."

"I'm not leaving, Frannie. We have to talk."

"What do you want after all this time? Did she finally smarten up and dump you?"

He shot me a look. His eyes narrowed and his mouth twitched as though my words had hit a nerve. I was right. That was exactly what had happened and he thought he could come back to me.

"Who was that guy?" he asked, deceptively soft.

I knew he was referring to Colton, but I didn't want to say his name in front of Chris. I didn't want to ever associate Colton with this monster.

"I. Said. Leave." I held his eyes and swallowed the bile rising in my throat.

I anticipated his next move because of instinct. He'd done it so many times before. He reached for my wrist, but I twisted out of the way. I managed to tap three numbers on my phone before he knocked it out of my hand.

He moved toward me again, but I jumped on my bed and out of his reach. His face turned red. "I asked you a question, Frannie. Who was that guy?"

"It's none of your business," I shouted back at him. He blocked the exit and cornered me in front of my bed and next to the dresser. I was trapped. Air emptied from my lungs and I could hardly breathe.

"It's my fucking business when a guy looks at me like I'm stepping on his territory. And you belong to me. You got that?"

"Nobody owns me, Chris. Especially not you." Despite my fear, a tiny spark of joy ignited in my heart at finally saying the words I had always wanted to say to him.

"Look. It wasn't serious with that other girl, Frannie. I'm willing to admit it was a mistake, but I'm back now and any other bullshit you have going on is over." He shouted those last words at me, using his usual tactics to frighten me. My body shuddered, but I tried to ignore it and speak clearly despite my physical reaction to him.

"No. What's over is us, Chris. I should have ended it years earlier, but I was too afraid. Now get out of my way."

"No. Not until you understand my side, what I went through."

"I will never see it your way. Don't you get it? I will never forgive you for what you did to me."

"I never touched you!" he shouted. "Do you know what some other guys do to their girls? I never once laid a hand on you, even though I could have."

What kind of monster said such a thing? Yes, he had never hit me, but I knew after all these years that his degrading words and actions had abused me, nonetheless. "Get out. You disgust me."

"I disgust you?" He took two steps and stood right in front of my face. "You pathetic little bitch!"

Something inside me snapped at his words. I couldn't take it anymore. My hands shook at my sides. I wouldn't allow him to make me feel less than again. *Enough*!

I smacked him hard against his cheek. His eyes went wild as his face grew red. Fear seized my lungs and I couldn't breathe. I wheezed in a breath right before he grabbed me and threw me on the bed. I kicked and punched and screamed, but he returned my earlier smack with one of his own. *Crack!*

My cheek burned and I wasn't sure what stung more, his hand or my humiliation. He had never hit me before, but I had always feared it. I hated him.

I hated how he made me feel worthless. Hated him for putting me in this situation again.

I hated him for being stronger and using that against me. Hated that he could.

Closing my eyes, I screamed, "Damn you!" Every muscle in my

body shook. "I hate you. I fucking hate you!" My throat burned from my violent outburst.

I struggled to push him off of me, but he held my arms above my head and straddled me. I knew he was stronger, but I also learned some self-defense in the years since walking away from Chris. Ramming my knee into his groin, I pushed my palm up against his chin. He fell beside the bed and I scrambled to get away from him. *When he's down, you run.* I recalled my instructor's voice drilling into us. I was nearly at the door when he grabbed my ankle. I pulled, but he gripped me tightly. Dropping to the ground, I used my other leg to kick him in the face. *Go for the nose, it's the easiest thing to break*, the voice reminded me.

"Ow!" he hollered and held his nose as blood sprayed between his fingers.

A siren blared outside my window, and my adrenaline soared. I ran down the stairs and threw open the front door, panting, just as a police cruiser pulled into my driveway. Two officers raced up my front steps as I dropped to my knees.

"Ma'am, are you all right?" asked the female officer when she reached me. "Is there someone inside?"

Nodding, I pointed up the stairs behind me. The officers drew their guns and cautiously walked up the steps. Chris stood at the top of the stairs with his hands up, blood smeared across his face, dripping down onto his flannel shirt.

"Hands behind your head," yelled the male officer. Chris dropped to his knees and brought his hands behind his head. He stared at me the whole time and I didn't dare turn away. My body shook, this time in anger, as I staggered to stand. Holding onto the door, I walked to the stairs, my hands shaking beside me. "Don't ever come near me again," I hissed.

His brow furrowed, and his mouth tilted into a frown. "You called the cops, Frannie," he sneered when the officer cuffed him.

"I should have called them a long time ago," I whispered as they shoved him past me and through the front door.

"Ma'am, we're going to need a statement. Can you drive to the station?" asked the female officer. As I shook my head, a black car came to a screeching halt in front of my house. It was Colton. The driver's door flew open, and he jumped out.

Rushing past the police officer, he hollered across the lawn, "What happened? Are you hurt?" His eyes were wild, scanning my body, perhaps looking for an injury, right before he pulled me into his arms.

"What are you doing here?" I whispered.

He cupped the back of my head while bending to speak softly in my ear. "I got your message but didn't want to respond by text. I wanted to see your face and talk to you in person."

"Sir, can you drive her to the station?" asked the officer.

"Yes, I can do that. I'll follow you." Turning to me, he asked, "Is that all right with you, Frances?"

I nodded and followed him to his car. We didn't exchange another word, not even when the tears came. Closing my eyes, I let the terror drain from my body and spill from my eyes.

Finally, when we neared the station, he ventured. "Who did this to you?" he asked.

My throat clogged up and I could barely swallow. I wanted to tell him, but the name would not come out. It was as though I couldn't sully his car with that filth.

"Was it your piece-of-shit ex?"

I smiled faintly because his words were exactly my sentiments.

Then, gripping the steering wheel, he whispered, "I'm going to fucking kill him."

His words should have disgusted me, or at the very least frightened me, but they didn't. They validated my own sentiments and normalized them. I hated Chris and I wanted to hurt him the way he had hurt me. If that made me a bad person, then I was tired of being good.

"I spent five years doubting myself, thinking I couldn't make it on my own in this world. Then, when I left, I hid behind my thoughts and my insecurities. I gave him five years. After today, I'm not wasting another five minutes on him."

"He didn't deserve you. That's why he made you feel less than because he could never rise to your level." He quickly turned to me before looking back at the road. "Never think otherwise."

Dr. Lee said I should face my fears. She probably hadn't imagined this, but after living through my worst nightmare and surviving it, a part of me finally started to believe that I was strong enough to deal with whatever came next.

Colton held my hand while the police took my statement. Whenever it trembled, he would caress my skin with his thumb until I was calm. I pressed charges that night and knew there would be a battle up ahead, but I was ready for it this time.

Climbing into Colton's car, I dropped my head back on the headrest. "Can I come to your place?" I asked. "I don't want to be alone in my house tonight. I won't get any sleep thinking about what happened."

"*Sweetheart*, I didn't know how to ask you that myself." He placed his hand on my knee and squeezed.

I turned toward the window and watched the light from the streetlamps dance. "I want you to hold me until the sun comes up," I whispered.

He cursed softly under his breath. "Then I'll stop the sun from rising."

And just like that, I smiled through the darkness.

***

The full moon guided the concrete path leading to his front door.

I kicked off my shoes this time when I entered, but before I could take another step, Colton swept me off my feet. Wrapping my arms around his neck and laying my head on his chest, I allowed him to carry me upstairs.

He set me down on white porcelain floors in what had to be the largest bathroom I'd ever seen. Walking toward a clawfoot tub with brass knobs, he turned on the water. I had considered taking a shower on the way here, but a bath now sounded much better.

"I'll give you a few minutes," he said as he tried to walk past me. I stopped him with a hand on his bicep.

"Stay," I said.

He watched me, waited for me to change my mind, perhaps. But I unbuttoned my blouse instead. His eyes followed my fingers as though I held them by a string. I let the blouse fall off my shoulders and unhooked my bra.

"Frances." His voice was hoarse, probably from when he had shouted earlier.

When not a stitch of clothing was left on my body, I walked slowly to the tub. Turning my head to look over my shoulder, I asked, "Will you join me?"

He shook his head. "I don't know what you're asking of me."

"I'm just asking you to hold me tonight, Colton."

He nodded. "I can do that."

The water engulfed my foot and the warmth ran up my leg. As I lay down in the tub, I watched Colton undress. Every time we had been together, it was dark and I could only think how badly I'd wanted him inside me. Now, I wanted to savor the moment and breathe in every part of him.

He tore off his white shirt first, his ridged abdomen clenching as he pulled his sleeves off his toned arms. The water sluiced over my thighs as I sank deeper into the tub. Then he unzipped his pants and dropped them to the floor. Despite his silence, it was now obvious how much he wanted me. "I'm sorry," he said. "It has a mind of its own."

I smiled. "It's all right. I don't mind." I pushed myself back from the tub and let him climb in behind me. Laying back against his chest, I closed my eyes when he wrapped his arms around me. I exhaled deeply and let the water and Colton's body cover me completely.

Taking a cloth next to the tub and adding soap to it, he ran the soft cotton along my arms and across my breasts. I closed my eyes and let him clean me. The soap glided across my knee, down my calf, then back up my thigh. I stretched my body like a cat as his movements massaged my tired muscles.

When he brought the cloth to my cheek, the one that Chris had slapped earlier, I flinched. The pain was still raw; the flesh bruised. He moved the cloth onto the other cheek and blended my tears with the bathwater. I hadn't realized I was crying until he asked me not to cry. Said it broke his heart. It broke mine too.

Water sloshed out of the tub when Colton stood. Grabbing a bath towel, he wrapped it around me as I stepped out of the bath. "I've got you," he said

He carried me to the bed this time, and lay beside me, holding me in his arms. I watched the full moon through his bedroom window until I saw only a sliver of it through my sleepy eyes.

23

Colton

The buzzing wouldn't stop. At first, I thought it was just my ears from the hurricane of thoughts swirling in my mind. But when the ping went off, I realized it was a phone. France's phone. She lay sleeping next to me and I didn't want to wake her, but the incessant noise surely would if I didn't turn it off.

Unzipping her purse, I pulled out her phone. Marco and Erika had called several times and left thirteen messages. I texted Erika that Frances was with me and everything was fine. I called Marco back.

"Hello? Frances? Are you all right?"

"It's Colton Crawford. I was the one that texted you from Frances's phone last night."

"I know who you are. Why are you calling me and not Frances? Is she hurt?"

I rubbed the back of my neck, thinking of the right words that wouldn't send him into a panic. Watching Frances buried underneath my black comforter and sheets, I told him the truth. "She's fine. She had a run-in with Chris and called the police. I took her to the station and brought her back to my place last night after she asked me to."

"Chris? Did he hurt her? I'll kill him."

I was proud of the boy's loyalty. "I'll take care of Chris," I assured him. "After my lawyers are finished with him—if he ever gets out of prison—I promise you, he'll never come near her again."

"Why can't I talk to her?" Marco asked.

"Because she's sleeping," I shot back.

A groggy voice called from the bed, "I *was* sleeping."

"I'm sorry," I said. "It's your brother. Do you want to speak with him?"

"Yeah." She pushed herself up on the bed and extended her hand for the phone. "Marco?"

"Yeah. I'm fine," she said, and pushed her hair away from her face. "Just tell them I'm fine and will be home this afternoon... I'll explain everything later... Okay, love you too."

She looked up at me. "I'm just going to call Mariam and let her know I'll be home today."

"Sounds good. I'll make coffee. I think we both need it."

I thanked the invention of coffee pods and quickly brewed two cups. When I returned to my bedroom, I gulped at the view in front of me. It wasn't the city landscape or the wide lake that caught my breath. It was her. Her brown curls spilled over my pillow. The outline of her body through the thin sheet drew my eyes to every womanly curve. I had imagined her in my bed before, but the reality was more beautiful than the fantasy.

I placed the mugs on the nightstand, then crawled in beside her.

She rested her head on my bare chest, her smooth cheek warming my cool skin. I sat holding her in my arms, content to never leave this room again, when she whispered, "He never hit me before."

Every muscle in my body tensed at the mention of violence toward her, and unconsciously I held her closer. "You don't have to talk about it," I said, smoothing a curl that wrapped around my forearm. "And one time is too many."

"He never hit me, but I always feared that he would. He would raise his hand and act like I'd pushed him too far. Or he'd scream in my face until his spit ran down my cheeks."

Every word she spoke pushed the tip of a blade deeper into my heart. Prison was too easy for the bastard.

"One day, after I told him I'd joined the young business chapter in my college, he threw me in the bedroom closet and pushed a chair in front of the door so I couldn't get out. He said it was to protect me that I was too naïve to know what really happened at college groups. He shouted that I was only trying to make him jealous and it had worked. I was trapped in there for six hours."

"Jesus, Frances." I ran both hands through my hair to stop myself from pushing off the bed and running after him. "I'm glad you never told me any of this before. I would have locked him in some dark place for days."

She pressed her lips to my chest before she continued. "That's why I hate dark places. And the reason I can't handle being smothered. I felt powerless and scared. Until recently, I hated my thoughts and closing myself off, but it made me feel safe. Does that even make sense?"

Tucking her head under my chin, I said, "You did what you had to do to get over the trauma. No one, especially not me, judges you for it."

"You're not scared of anything," she mumbled.

I snorted a sarcastic laugh. "Oh, Frances. You're so wrong."

On the dresser in front of my bed sat a photo of my brothers and me with our parents, two weeks before they died. My heart pounded and the memory made me shiver.

"I'm terrified of trusting people. I'm scared I'll trust someone and they will hurt the people I love."

She rubbed her fingers along my forearm, warming up the goosebumps that had risen on my flesh. "What happened?" she asked.

"It's a long story," I said.

"I've got nowhere to go." She snuggled closer to my body, strumming her fingers along the ridges of my stomach.

"When my parents passed away, my uncle and aunt took us in. He was my dad's brother but we had spent little time with him. Maybe I saw him at Christmas. It didn't matter. I was so relieved that someone would take us in and they wouldn't separate us in foster homes that I didn't care how often we had seen him before, just as long as we were all together now.

"After they moved in with us, they weren't around much. My brothers and I had to fend for ourselves. It didn't bother me, but Ryan questioned it a lot. Wondered why they would even bother taking us in. I told him to stop being ungrateful and just be happy we weren't on the streets or worse."

"That sounds pretty reasonable to me," she said.

Recalling several conversations with my brothers when we were younger, I added, "They never saw it that way. Luke would beg our uncle to watch him play baseball after school, but he always declined."

I ran my fingers along her back while my mind drifted to one particular memory.

*

The August sun blared down the windows and sucked all the air from inside the playroom. Beads of sweat gathered on my forehead, but I hardly noticed. I was too busy building a skyscraper with Lego.

My uncle walked in and I held still, wondering what Luke and I had done now and how to fix it. But the words that came out of his mouth shocked me.

"It's a hot one out there. A good day to go for ice cream. What do you think, Colton?" he asked. If he hadn't addressed me, I would have thought he was speaking to someone else. My uncle had never offered to take us anywhere.

"I think that's a good idea," I replied, cautiously.

"Wonderful," he exclaimed, then clapped his hands once. "Well, get up, boy. The ice cream won't come to you. We'll drive there."

I stumbled to my feet, rushing to stand. "Thank you," I said. "I'll go grab Luke. I think Ryan's at a friend's house, but I can call him."

"No need," he said, putting his hand on my shoulder to stop me from leaving the room. "It will be just the two of us."

I hesitated but didn't want to blow the chance that my uncle was finally coming around. And maybe he would ask all three of us next time, so I agreed.

When we reached the ice cream shop, he let me choose three flavors, and when I brought that ice cream cone to my mouth, it was taller than my ten-year-old face.

"Listen, Colton," he said, sitting in a steel chair in front of me, with no ice cream cone in his hands. "Your aunt would like to wear something of your mother's to remember her by. Can you open the safe for us?"

My entire body froze and it wasn't from the cold dessert. A niggling voice in my head warned me not to give it to him. "I… I… don't know the code."

He smiled. "Sure, you do. Your daddy always said how smart you are and how you'll take over the business one day. You're telling me you never figured out a tiny thing like the code?"

I didn't have to figure it out. My mother had given it to me. I would fetch her earrings and bracelets before she'd go out for the night. But he didn't know that. At least I didn't think he did. So, I shook my head.

"Do you like staying in your house, Colton? Do you enjoy living with your brothers and attending the same school you've always attended? It would be a shame if your aunt and I couldn't support you any longer."

I knew my parents had left them a sizable income as our

caregivers, but he could pull us out of school and make our lives miserable. "Why would you do that to us?" I asked.

"Because you're acting very ungrateful right now. I'm simply asking to borrow a trinket for a night. That isn't too much to ask, considering how much we've done for you and your brothers. Is it, Colton?"

*

Frances's voice pulled me from the memory. "That's terrible," she whispered.

The familiar sense of self-disgust washed over me. "No. What's terrible is that I gave him the code. I told myself to trust him because he was family. But I just wanted him to care about us, not abandon us. I was too afraid to do it on my own."

Sitting up, facing me, she asked, "What happened next?"

I stared at the white wall in front of me, but I only saw the black empty safe in my mother's closet, and my heart hurt all over again as it did that day. "I checked the safe the next day and it was all gone. Everything. The jewelry, the ownership of the cars and boats my parents owned.

"I asked him when he would return them and he said to leave him alone and not be a brat or he'd kick us out. I swore to myself that as soon as I turned eighteen, I'd take me and my brothers away from him and I would retrieve every piece he had stolen from us."

"Did you get the jewelry back?"

"No. When I turned eighteen, I pressed the bastard up against a wall with my bare hands and demanded that he return my mother's jewels. I didn't care about the cars and yachts; I could replace those, but I knew how much my mother loved those pieces. They were heirlooms and she'd wanted to pass them on to her children."

Clenching my fist, I still found it difficult to say this last part. "He said he'd sold every piece and didn't have one left. I believed him. They lived a lavish lifestyle and the jewels wouldn't have been enough to sustain them." My throat seized, but I finished what I had to say aloud, "It breaks my heart knowing that whatever is left of my mother is scattered around in pieces."

Her soft fingers squeezed my hand. "You were just a little boy. You have to know that."

"It doesn't matter. I was the one that gave him the code. I won't stop until I've found every piece."

"You've located some of them?"

"Yes. I have a private investigator helping me. We've found sets all over the world at auctions or estate sales. There's just one more still missing."

"That's incredible, Colton."

"It's taken nearly twenty years. But yes, I'm almost there."

Nodding her head, she said softly, "That's why you were so upset with me. It's why you didn't even let me explain."

"I should have let you explain. But, yes, my pride got in the way. I couldn't believe I'd allowed someone to deceive me again."

But that wasn't what I was most sorry about. "I should never have allowed Ryan to hire an investigator to look into you. I'm sorry. I'd wanted to prove to him and myself that I hadn't done it again. But life has a way of making you face your fears even when you think you can't."

"I get why you were so angry now," she said. "I'm sorry I proved to be as false as your uncle."

"God, don't ever say that. You're nothing like him. You lied to help your brother, not to swindle something out of me."

"Well... I did swindle a job out of you," she said with a laugh. I loved hearing her laugh. It made the weight of my past feel less heavy. "*Woman*, you can take whatever you want from me—whenever you want it—from now on. I'll give it to you freely."

She stretched her leg over mine and crawled on top of my body. She wore a white t-shirt. Her nipples, visible through the cotton fabric, beckoned me. I couldn't resist, so I put my mouth to one and licked. Pulling me closer to her, she moaned, and my cock stiffened. I wanted her so badly, wanted to throw her down on the bed and push myself deep inside of her. But I commanded myself to be patient and let her take the lead.

Her fingers skimmed down my arms and across my chest. She palmed my hard cock through my gray sweatpants. It was pure torture. Leaning my head back on the bed, I willed my hands to stay still. She'd been through enough yesterday. She didn't need me pawing all over her. I would only take what she was willing to give and I wouldn't complain. At least not aloud. In my head, I was fucking screaming.

Her fingers moved to the hem of her shirt, lifting it up and over her head. I stared at her breasts. I knew I should look at her face, but my neck wouldn't move. My eyes were glued to the mounds in front of me. Burying my face between them, I thought I'd die a lucky man here. When she pushed my head lower, I leaped at her invitation and laid her down on the bed. I ran my lips down below her stomach, inhaling the scent of her.

"The taste of you, the sounds you make. It all drives me crazy. All it takes is one touch from you, and I'm lost," I said.

She whispered my name, and she may have said something else, but she covered my ears when she grasped my head between the palms of her hands. I feasted on her, licking her from her lips down to her core. I circled her clit with my tongue until she squirmed in my hands.

Spreading her thighs further apart, I held her while she screamed my name. Pushing down my pants, I grabbed a hold of myself and pumped to relieve some of the pressure. It hurt how badly I needed her. Naked, with her thighs still spread open for me, I guided my cock to her entrance. Nudging against her, I teased her until she wet her lips.

"I don't think I can come again after that," she said, and I grinned at the challenge.

"I wasn't trying to make you come yet, *sweetheart*, just getting you ready for me."

I licked her nipples, circling them with my tongue while my thumb did the same to her clit. She groaned, raking her nails against my back. When I felt her entrance open wider for me, I nudged a little further inside. This time, I was the one who groaned. "You feel so good."

Raising myself onto one hand, I used the other to pleasure her. Pushing deeper inside her, I moved until I hit her spot. "There," she whispered.

Her moaning got louder and my cock got harder. I listened to her breathing, hearing her excitement grow with every pant. When she clenched the sheets between her fingers, I knew she was close, and so was I.

"Colton," she cried. "Please, don't stop."

Never. I kept the same rhythm and angle, pumping in and out of her on my knees, holding my body high above her. Her thighs quivered and she arched her back, her mouth forming an 'O'. It was the most beautiful sight, knowing I was the one giving her pleasure.

Then, her breathing became frantic, and she screamed my name once more, just as her body spasmed underneath me. Knowing she had reached her climax, I let my instincts take over. I pounded harder, making her reach back and hold on to the headboard until my release finally rocked me and I shouted her name.

Falling onto the bed next to her, I was completely spent. My harsh breaths were all I heard until a faint chuckle tickled my ear. I turned my head to look at her, she rested on her side, one arm cradled beneath her head.

"Now that was quite the make-up sex," she said.

I laughed and pulled her close against me. "That wasn't make-up sex, *sweetheart*. I'll give that to you every night. All you've got to do is take that t-shirt off again."

24

Frances

The steam from the shower covered the glass walls and surrounded me, blanketing me in its warmth. The hot water hit the top of my head and I stood still, letting it drip down my neck, then my arms and legs. I watched the water create new pathways on my skin. I imagined it erasing my fears, my past, my present, leaving a blank space for me to write my future.

A cold gust of air made me shiver, and I turned toward it. Colton stood naked on the other side with a shit-eating grin. I laughed but shook my head. "Oh, no you don't. I'm done and getting out now."

He groaned. "I promise to clean you myself afterward."

His cock twitched with eagerness, and my core clenched. I stepped to the side and he quickly joined me under the nozzle. Pulling me into his arms, I closed my eyes and enjoyed the feel of his hands all over my body.

His fingers tickled down my back and I lifted my head, reaching for his lips. He kissed me and lifted me by the back of my thighs. Curling my legs around his hips, I held on as tightly as I could. He guided himself into me and I moaned next to his ear in pleasure. He squeezed my ass and pushed me in deeper. I never wanted to shower alone again.

I rode his body furiously, and the tension built quickly this time. Perhaps it was the heat from the steam that relaxed my muscles, or that my body was primed for him, but I came faster than I'd thought possible. Even Colton looked surprised. I laughed at his grin and climbed down from his body.

He bit his lip and I bent down to grab the soap. He groaned and I held back my giggle. Lathering the soap between my hands, I placed them on his solid stomach and rubbed the suds along his body until I reached for his cock. He dropped his head back and licked his lips. I couldn't help but lick my own.

He grabbed my hands and rubbed his fingers between my soapy ones, and then curled them inside of me, washing me as he'd promised earlier.

My flesh was still sensitive, so I rose onto my tiptoes, holding onto him as he lathered me. When I couldn't take it anymore, I dropped to my knees, letting the water fall onto my back while I took Colton into my mouth.

"Frances," he whispered. "Oh, god."

I had never enjoyed sex until I met Colton. Had never really experienced pleasure before. I'd just wanted it to be over as quickly as possible. But now, I knew how much more there could be, and I wanted it all.

I swept my tongue along his smooth tip and hallowed my cheeks to suck harder. He threw a hand up against the wet tiled wall and curved his body forward. I felt powerful, knowing this beautiful, strong man was weak for me right now. Grabbing onto his cheeks, I pushed harder until I felt him at the back of my throat. He growled and pulled my face away while he spent himself in the water.

His chest heaved and he panted, sucking in air. He laughed when he saw my grin. "Proud of yourself, aren't you?"

"A little," I said with a wink.

"Well, you should be. I'll need a minute before I can walk."

"Take all the time you need. I'm going to dry off."

I couldn't find a blow dryer in any of his bathroom drawers. "Do you have any hair products?" I called back.

"What?" he shouted, his head underneath the nozzle.

"Never mind," I said, finding a tube of gel at the back of the cupboard. "This should work." I hoped it would at least keep the worst of my frizzies away.

I had finished dressing when Colton finally turned the water off. I padded around his room until I reached the dresser. Staring at a framed family photo, something caught my attention. I picked up the frame and examined it closer.

I recognized Colton's eyes despite him being a very young boy in this photo. Ryan and Luke stood on either side of him. His mother was exceptionally beautiful, so beautiful that one wonders if she were even real. But that's not what made me stare at her. Examining the gold necklace she wore, I realized something—I'd seen it before.

Oh my god!

"Colton!" I shouted. "Colton!"

He ran from the bathroom in black jeans, no shirt, his black hair still wet. "Are you okay?"

My hand holding the photo shook while the other one covered my mouth. "Is this the last piece of jewelry? The one you haven't found yet?"

"Yes. Why?"

I dropped my arm but clutched the picture in my hand. "I think I know where it is."

***

I gripped the passenger seat as Colton sped down the freeway toward my neighborhood. "Colton, you're going really fast," I said.

My shoulders slumped forward as the car slowed down.

"I'm sorry," he said, his eyes trained on the road. The palm of his hand rubbed his thigh as we approached a traffic light.

"We're almost there," I reassured him. "It's almost over."

He nodded and hit the gas when the light turned green, jerking my head back.

He pulled into the plaza at the corner of my street. He hadn't jumped out of the car as I'd expected him to do. Instead, he stared through the windshield at the black gated door leading to the pawnshop.

Inhaling deeply, he turned to me. "I'm ready." I wasn't sure if he was trying to convince me or himself.

We walked to the front entrance and the familiar bell chimed as I opened the door. A middle-aged man wearing a leather motorcycle jacket was the only other customer in the shop. He stood in front of the glass case that held the necklace the last time I was here. "It was just over there," I said, tilting my head toward the older man.

"Thanks, Jim," said the shopkeeper as he handed the man a white plastic bag. "See you next time."

As the man ambled past us, he looked at Colton, giving him a once over, but Colton ignored him and moved toward the spot I'd indicated earlier. The door chimed again, and I joined Colton at the counter.

"I don't see it," he said, scanning the pieces below. I quickly raked my gaze across the cabinet, and when I couldn't find it either, I walked over to the next one, hoping the owner had simply moved it. But it wasn't there.

"I saw a gold necklace here a few weeks ago. It had an emerald in it. It was right here," I said, pointing at the spot I'd seen it last.

"Just sold it," said the shopkeeper. "But I've got other pieces I can show you."

"What do you mean by 'just'?" Colton asked, his voice level, but his pulled eyebrows showed his frustration.

"Just a couple of minutes ago," he explained. "But I got this piece in today. I haven't even put it on display yet."

"I don't want another piece," said Colton, stopping the shopkeeper. "Do you mean the biker?"

The man hesitated, but his eyes looked up behind us. Following his gaze, Colton turned toward the entrance. The man straddled his bike and was putting on his helmet as Colton ran outside. We chased after him, but all we caught was the loud engine and the dust left behind from the man speeding away.

Dammit!

I turned to comfort Colton, but he grabbed my hand and pulled me toward his car. "We're going after him," he said.

"What? Are you crazy?"

"Maybe." He started the engine. "But I haven't searched this long to just let it go now." He peeled out onto the road in the same direction as the biker. Fortunately, it was a long street and I spotted the motorcycle about four blocks ahead of us.

"There," I said, pointing to the bike.

"I see him." Colton swerved to the left, passing the car in front. The bike was only three blocks ahead of us now.

"What are you going to say when you reach him?" I asked, hoping this would not turn into some brawl.

"I don't know. I guess it depends on him."

"That's what I was afraid of," I murmured.

The bike made a left turn at the next intersection and we followed closely. Only two blocks separated us at this point. When he pulled into some dive bar, my stomach dropped, but Colton didn't take his foot off the pedal.

He pulled up next to the bike just as the man removed his helmet. He recognized us immediately and crossed his arms as he watched us get out of the car.

"What's your problem, man? Why are you following me?" he asked.

"You purchased a necklace at the pawnshop. I want to buy it

back from you," Colton explained. That wasn't so bad. It sounded reasonable.

"It's not for sale," said the man.

Ugh! Come on!

"Look," began Colton, walking closer to the guy. "This piece you bought has sentimental value to me. You can buy something else with the money."

"Well, my old lady, she likes this antique stuff, so I'm thinking it'll have some sentimental value to her, too."

Colton rubbed his face and blew out a frustrated sigh. "How much do you want?"

The man raised his bushy salt-and-pepper eyebrows and snuck a glance at the black sports car behind us. "I'm thinking five grand."

What!

"Done," said Colton, surprising me with his quick response.

The man grinned. "Did I say five? I meant ten."

Nodding, Colton stared down at the pavement right before he reached across and grabbed the man by his t-shirt collar.

"I know I may look like some spoiled shit, but let's get one thing clear. I'm not a fool." They stared at one another, neither willing to back down.

"Ah, Colton?" I interrupted.

"Yeah?"

"About ten guys are standing out front of the bar right now, watching you."

Colton's head snapped up and the man smiled. I wasn't sure about Colton, but the weathered faces of the men behind us scared me.

"We should go," I said when I saw a few of the men approaching us.

"I'm not leaving without that necklace." Colton still held the man by his shirt. "What's it going to be? Will you take the five grand and buy your old lady whatever she damn well pleases or do I sue you and your friends for assaulting me and I bring this whole fucking place down?"

The man stared pointedly at Colton's fist. Letting go, Colton stepped back. The biker straightened his t-shirt and leather jacket and held up his hand when his friends were only a few feet behind us. I held my breath, afraid even the slightest movement would tilt the outcome of this standoff.

"Do you have the money on you?" asked the scary biker dude.

"No. But I can transfer it to you right now."

"All right. Go ahead. It's maddawg69@lolo.com."

Grabbing his phone, Colton punched in his email address.

"It's done." He extended his hand forward, with his palm open. "Now, give me the necklace."

The biker grabbed a phone from the back of his bike and pressed a finger to the screen. After a few minutes, he finally reached back into the bike's compartment and retrieved the white plastic bag.

Colton pulled his hand back, as though afraid to touch the bag. "Frances, can you check if that's the necklace you saw in the photograph?" he asked, still staring at the biker's outstretched arm.

Gently taking the bag from the biker's grasp as though any sudden movement would change his mind, I peeked inside. "Yes, it's the same one."

Colton nodded, but I noticed his throat working up and down.

"Hope she's worth it," said the biker, looking over at me. I blushed, knowing the necklace wasn't for me. It had nothing to do with us. But Colton surprised me when he responded, "She's worth way more than that."

My heart leaped at his words. I didn't know if it was bravado or if he had truly meant them. Regardless, he stole my heart with those six words, and I didn't know if I'd ever get it back.

As we drove out of the lot, I was too reluctant to mention it, so I ignored what he'd said and focused on the necklace. "Did you want to look at it?"

"Not yet," he said. "I want to be at home when I do."

He drove much more slowly than he had before, stopping at every yellow light and barely hitting the speed limit. When he pulled into his driveway and turned off the ignition, he let out a loud sigh and turned toward me.

"Can you show it to me, please?"

My heart pounded in my chest. For a moment, I panicked, wondering if I'd been mistaken. It looked just like the necklace his mother had worn, but was it the same one?

The gold felt frigid in my hands, the smooth metal sliding between my fingers. I lifted the necklace and let it dangle in front of him. "Is this the one?"

He reached for it, turning the piece back and forth until he brought his eyes closer to the clasp. Pulling his lips into his mouth, he inhaled sharply through his nose, then exhaled a loud breath through his lips.

"Are you all right, Colton?" I asked when he rubbed his eyes with the heel of his hands.

His voice was raw, as though each word scraped the back of his throat. "It's finally over," he said. "It's finally finished."

"Your search?" I asked.

"My penance."

The pain in his eyes cut through my chest and squeezed my heart. This man had blamed himself for something someone else had done to him. But not anymore. "You did it, Colton. You've recouped every piece that your uncle stole from you and your brothers. Now you have everything you've always wanted."

He closed his eyes, and when he opened them, they burned with an intensity I felt in the pit of my stomach. It tossed my insides around until I could hardly breathe. "Not everything," he said. "I want you, Frances. Not just today, but every day. I want you in my office, in my bed, in my life."

I inhaled sharply, unsure of how to react to his words. They excited me. They enchanted me, but mostly they overwhelmed me. The thought of being with Colton, no lie stopping us, no past holding us back. It was too much—he was too much. And in the past, well, I never felt like I was enough.

But not anymore.

My old insecurities still rustled in my head, but I was tired of letting them control me. I'd come so far in the last few months, there was no reason I couldn't go much further—especially now that I wanted more. I thought a powerful CEO like Colton could never fall for a mailroom girl like me. It wasn't my job that held me back, but the limitations I'd placed on myself.

I wanted Colton. I wanted him in my life too, and I was done being afraid that I wouldn't be good enough. I was enough—for him and for me.

Placing my hand on his cheek, I slowly brought my lips to his. "Take me home," I whispered against them. His gaze dropped, and he nodded. I smiled, realizing he didn't understand what I'd meant. So, when I brushed my thumb across his bottom lip, I added, "Take me back to your place."

His breath hitched, and his eyes heated right before he devoured my lips.

25

Frances

Two weeks later, my blue heels clicked against the white marble floor of Crawford Corporation. My gray pencil skirt and gray blazer blended perfectly with the other suits as I walked toward the elevator. Three of us entered at the same time, and I found myself at the back.

"Twelfth floor, please," I called out to the man in front. When he turned to look at me, I recognized him as the same man in the navy suit who had ignored me several months ago. He smiled and pressed the button for the twelfth floor.

"I guess you can hear just fine then," I said when the doors closed.

"I'm sorry," he asked. "Do I know you?"

I shook my head. "Not at all."

All right, that wasn't exactly true, but I felt like a different person. It certainly was a new beginning for me.

As I waited for the elevator doors to open, my phone pinged. Checking the message, I noticed it was from Marco.

Marco: Hey, my first class was amazing. I learned some cool new design tricks. This graphics course will be killer but worth it. Luv you, sis.

My heart swelled and I smiled down at the phone. I was so proud of my little brother and happy I could help him.

Me: Can't wait to hear all about it later. Nonna's making your favorite for dinner, gnocchi.

Marco: 😊

"Hey there, girl," said Erika when I approached her desk. "Nice to see you back at the office."

"It's good to see you, too." I walked around the desk and hugged her.

"Are we still getting lunch together today?" she asked.

"Definitely," I said, pointing a finger at her new headband. "There's a lot I want to discuss with you."

She grinned. "Looking forward to it."

"Is he in?" I asked.

"Yep. Hasn't left his office all day."

I nodded and walked toward Colton's office.

I spotted Ava Grady at her desk, typing away. I inhaled a deep breath and marched toward her.

"Hi, Ava," I said, and kept my hands rigid next to my sides. I didn't want to fidget or appear nervous despite my rising anxiety. I was getting better, but I still wasn't completely over my fear of confrontation.

She swiveled in her chair, crossed her arms, and raised her eyebrows at me in anticipation. Okay, she wouldn't make this easy.

"I wanted to apologize to you personally for what I did." She continued to stare at me. "I had no right to take the PA job under false pretense and assume your identity, even if it was only to be temporary. I meant you no harm, but it was still wrong of me to do so. I'm truly sorry."

She stood and uncrossed her arms. "That was pretty unprofessional if not downright unlawful," she said, and my heart sped up, wondering if she would press charges. "But I can't help but have mad respect for a woman willing to go to great lengths to get what she wants. I won't make it easy for you if you want your job back. The pay is incomparable. I heard you negotiated that. Nice work."

"You're welcome," I said, and glimpsed Colton's white shirt and his hand rubbing the back of his neck. "See you around," I said to Ava and walked up to Colton's office.

"Frances, *sweetheart*," he said, looking up from his computer, already rising from his chair.

"Please, sit. We need to talk," I said.

"All right," he said, slowly. "I'm glad to see you. Did you want to take a seat here or go someplace else?" He gestured toward the black leather chair in front of his desk.

"Here's fine." I sat down on the chair, feeling the soft leather massage the back of my thighs. "You know, the first time I sat down here, I wondered how it would feel making love to you on it." Colton's eyes grew larger and he checked over my head in Ava's direction.

"Perhaps we can make that fantasy a reality," he whispered.

I smiled. "Perhaps, but that's not why I came here."

"Too bad," he said, and leaned back in his chair. "What's going on, Frances?"

"I quit my job at Sterling Realty this morning," I said. He leaned forward and placed his forearms on his desk. "You did? That's great." He smiled.

I raised my eyebrows. "It is?"

"Of course. I didn't know how to ask you to quit and come work for me, but you did it. I'm so relieved."

"What about Ryan? How does he feel about me working at Crawford Corp again?"

"Ryan never wanted me to fire you. He just wanted to get to the truth. He said he wants to apologize to you. I can call him up now if you wish."

"I don't need an apology from Ryan. I understand why he did it now. I know quite well how one's past can influence future decisions. I don't hold it against him anymore."

"That's such a relief, Frances," said Colton, sighing and running a hand through his dark hair. The movement still made my stomach do a little flip as it always had. "I'm sure once you start working here again, you'll get to know him."

"I do hope to get to know Ryan better, but it won't be through work. I didn't come here looking for a job, Colton."

He tilted his head, and worry creased his brow. "Then why did you come?"

I stood and placed a sheet of paper on his desk. "I came to tell you that I've started my own marketing business. Erika and Mrs. Morgan have hired me to help them with their ventures. It's time I put into practice what I studied and love to do—helping new businesses."

He looked down at the contract signed by Marie Morgan, the first for my new consulting company. "So, you won't be taking the job here?" he asked.

I shook my head, "No."

"And you'll be helping Marie Morgan, even though I still haven't heard which way they'll go with their property?"

I nodded, "Yes."

He stood and walked over, sitting on the edge of his desk with his arms crossed. I raised my chin to look him in the eye. I couldn't help but recall the moment I pretended to be Ava Grady and how different this felt. How in control I felt now.

"Do you love me?" he asked.

"Yes," I whispered. "With all my heart."

He nodded and pressed down on his lips. "I told you before that I want you, Frances. I want you beside me every day. Your smile would brighten up every room in this office, but I also love that you have your own dreams."

He pushed off his desk and walked toward the back cabinet. Grabbing his keys from his suit pocket, he unlocked the top drawer and pulled out a box. "I had big plans on how I would do this, but I can't wait any longer."

He walked toward me, his eyes seizing mine, as he dropped to one knee in the middle of his office. My hand flew to my mouth, catching my loud gasp. "Colton," I said, breathless, as he took my hand.

"From the moment I saw you standing there, you took my breath away. I was blind for not noticing you before, but I see you now. I love everything about you. You showed strength, courage, and grace throughout this entire ordeal, and I am humbled to kneel before you and ask you to be my wife." He opened the box. A gold and emerald ring with diamonds around it sparkled under the fluorescent light. "Frances, will you marry me?"

Although I'd never seen the ring before, it reminded me of the necklace we'd found. It must have been his mother's ring and now he offered it to me. What had once been stolen from him had been found, and I couldn't help feeling the same about myself. Chris had stolen my eagerness to love and be seen, but now that I'd found it again, I wanted to share my love with Colton.

"Yes." The word shot through my lips and I laughed at his relieved expression. "Yes, I'll marry you."

Standing, he cupped my face and took my lips in a fierce kiss. "I love you, Frances," he whispered when he moved his mouth to my jaw.

"I love you too." My voice held the passion I felt and the conviction Colton deserved.

With a low groan, he picked me up off the floor and held me in his arms. It felt like home. A new home, one we'd built together working through deceits, personal failures, and messy pasts.

I wanted to leave it all behind and start anew. But I had one more secret to share with him first.

"I wasn't expecting you to surprise me like this, especially when I had planned to do all the surprising. But there's one more thing I came here to tell you."

He put me down and watched my every move as I fetched an envelope from my purse. "Marie gave this to me this morning to pass along to you."

"What is it?"

"Open it."

He ripped open the envelope and the brilliant smile that spread across his face had me grinning from cheek to cheek. He rubbed a hand over his face to cover his joy, but he couldn't hide it from me.

"He signed it?"

I nodded enthusiastically. "It's yours. Morgan agreed to your plans and signed the papers today."

He dropped the paper and picked me up once again, this time spinning me around the room. "Congratulations, Colton. This is going to be your legacy."

He put me down and held my face. "No, *sweetheart*. This is just business. My love for you will be my legacy. I promise you that."

Then he kissed me until I forgot my own name—again.

***

Thank you for reading The Mix-Up! If you enjoyed Frances and Colton's story, please consider leaving a review.

If you enjoyed this book and would like to read my other stories, please visit my website.

Thank you for reading THE MIX-UP, and supporting indie authors!

Acknowledgment

A huge thank you:

To my husband and children, who supported this dream from the beginning.

To my alpha reader, Gilda, who is as passionate about finding errors as I am.

To my critique partners, Karhyll and Christine, your time and relentlessness are worth more to me than I can express.

To my writing friends Kandie, Anuja, Nita, Jayme, and Nadja, thank you for keeping the imposter syndrome down and my spirits up.

To my cover designer BetiBup, for their patience.

To the Facebook groups 20booksto50k and The Writing Gals who make indie publishing a little less scary.

Finally, to my readers. My heart will always belong to you. Your excitement and fierce love for my stories inspire me every day. From the bottom of my heart, thank you!

ABOUT THE AUTHOR

Eve Marian is a former journalist and public relations executive. She lives in a suburb of Toronto with her husband, two children, and a clever cat named Chase.

To receive the latest information on new releases, giveaways, promotions, and more, sign up for her newsletter at www.evemarian.com.

Other books by Eve Marian:

Billionaire Romance Series:
The Mix-Up
The Remake

Paranormal Romance Series:
VIOLET SKY Forbidden Love
VIOLET SKY Second Chances
VIOLET SKY Avenging Love

www.ingramcontent.com/pod-product-compliance
Lightning Source LLC
Chambersburg PA
CBHW030338310726
48979CB00001B/88

* 9 7 8 1 7 7 8 0 2 6 2 6 3 *